THE BODY

We followed Jimmy around the back of the building to the staff entrance. Instead of entering the museum, Jimmy turned right and unlocked another door that led into an adjacent hangar, where the plane restoration was done. The only light in the place was coming from the far end of the building.

"Jonas? It's Jimmy, the new guy you met this afternoon. It's late. Shouldn't you be knocking off soon?" he said loudly.

We heard no response.

"I'll bet he's in the flight simulator back there," Jimmy said to us, heading in that direction. "He was telling me today how he couldn't wait to get his pilot's license so he could take off whenever he wanted."

Our footsteps echoed in the dark cavern as Sally and I followed closely behind Jimmy. Darkness can make a lot of places creepy, but the shadows and partially illuminated propellers, wings and wheels of these old planes made me think I was being surrounded by decomposing dinosaurs. I finally relaxed when we reached the simulator capsule, but that was very short-lived.

"Ladies first," Jimmy said, and I climbed the metal steps to the cockpit entrance. Once my eyes adjusted to the light inside, I could take in the gruesome scene.

Sitting at the controls was a body I assumed was Jonas . . .

Books by Christine E. Blum

FULL BODIED MURDER
MURDER MOST FERMENTED
THE NAME OF THE ROSÉ

Published by Kensington Publishing Corporation

The Name of the Rosé

CHRISTINE E. BLUM

KENSINGTON BOOKS
www.kensingtonbooks.com

KENSINGTON BOOKS are published by

Kensington Publishing Corp.
119 West 40th Street
New York, NY 10018

All Kensington titles, imprints, and distributed lines are available at special quantity discounts for bulk purchases for sales promotion, premiums, fund-raising, educational, or institutional use.

Special book excerpts or customized printings can also be created to fit specific needs. For details, write or phone the office of the Kensington Sales Manager: Attn.: Sales Department. Kensington Publishing Corp., 119 West 40th Street, New York, NY 10018. Phone: 1-800-221-2647.

Kensington and the K logo Reg. U.S. Pat. & TM Off.

First Printing: December 2018
ISBN-13: 978-1-4967-1214-1
ISBN-10: 1-4967-1214-5

ISBN-13: 978-1-4967-1215-8 (ebook)
ISBN-10: 1-4967-1215-3 (ebook)

10 9 8 7 6 5 4 3 2 1

Printed in the United States of America

For Ofelia

Acknowledgments

I thank the Santa Monica Airport for its rich history and my endless fascination with what it can provide Los Angeles both in times of emergencies and not. May it never leave us. Thanks also to the Santa Monica police, and especially public service supervisor Leo Iniguez for the in-depth tour and anecdotes from his long tour of duty at the airport. I also want to give a big shout-out to the Aquarium of the Pacific in Long Beach, and especially aquarist Angelina Komatovich. If you're in the neighborhood be sure and pay them a visit. It is a fantastic place and they are doing such wonderful things.

This book is dedicated to Ofelia, who may or may not bear some resemblance to the character of Marisol. Ofelia may or may not have appointed herself the Mayor of Rose Avenue and may or may not like to spy on me. But one thing that I know for sure is that she has enriched my life greatly. Thank you.

CHAPTER 1

"I hope that wasn't a plane I heard crashing at the airport," Sally said.

"I heard it too as I went out to water the hibiscus," Aimee agreed, getting teary at the thought.

"Which I'm guessing you did in your baby doll nightie again? You're going to give old Keith across the street a heart attack one of these days." I laughed, knowing I was right.

"We'd have heard something by now if it was serious," Sally concluded. "Cheers!"

Ah, that magic Pavlovian word. At the sound of it, we all hoisted our glasses, looked each other in the eyes and clinked. The Rose Avenue Wine Club had begun.

We were imbibing at my house today. It was an uncharacteristically hot Thursday in June that demanded to be experienced al fresco around my pool. All the usual neighborhood suspects were in attendance. There was the aforementioned Sally, a statuesque African American woman with the long, elegant hands of a painter and the mouth, at times, of a truck driver. She is my closest Rose Avenue friend. Next up Aimee, our budding young entrepreneur and owner of the Chill Out frozen yogurt shop. Her Bambi eyes absorb the world and the people around her like a desert flower in the rain. Despite her cold workplace, she is far from being sangfroid. She wears her emotions on her sleeve, jeans, hair and just about every fiber of her being. Which is what makes her so endearing.

Peggy is pretty much her polar opposite: widowed, in her late eighties but strong-willed and quick-witted. In another century, I'm pretty sure if you walked past her house she'd be eyeing you from a porch rocking chair, clutching a shotgun resting across her knees. But she's also the great matriarch of numerous grandbabies, so a hug from her is better than hot chocolate with marshmallows on a cold day. Or a fine Napa Cabernet. Wait, maybe I've gone too far.

We were also honored to welcome Mary Ann Wallis to the fermented coterie. She's been a longtime neighbor but a new convert to the club. This may have to do with her decision to cut back on her journalist duties at the *Los Angeles Times* and stop to smell the rosés. I'd heard she'd been a powerhouse when she worked the beat, which is an even greater phenomenon, given that she's about five-foot-one and couldn't weigh more than one hundred pounds soaking wet. She's living proof the pen is mightier than the sword.

"I'm so used to the planes now that I only hear them if something sounds off: a sputtering engine or complete silence after takeoff. That noise was neither, so maybe everything's fine," Mary Ann said as I passed around a plate of heirloom radishes lightly coated in French butter and sea salt.

Please allow me to introduce myself. I'm Halsey, and I moved here from New York City after a divorce that should never have been a marriage. But that was almost three years ago, and I am firmly assimilated into life on Rose Avenue in this small Los Angeles beach community. I'd say that having been falsely suspected of committing two murders, being kidnapped, locked up in jail and left stranded in a fifteen-foot-deep trench counts in the dues-paying department.

I make my living writing code and designing websites, and when I started my company in New York during the tech bubble, I would never have imagined that I'd later be plying my trade from a suburban house on a Chinese elm–lined street with a converted garage for an office. So it goes. In addition to Wine Club, there's a guy; there's always a guy. Oh, don't misunderstand me: Jack is a great one and we actually met because of the true love of my life, my yellow Lab, Bardot. But let's just say my prior unfortunate affaire de coeur has left me a tad commitment phobic.

Just to finish the picture, I'm five-eight, blond, okay highlighted and thirty-six-years-old. Oh, and my given name is Annie Elizabeth Hall, but for obvious reasons, the moniker I answer to is Halsey, a nickname that stuck when I was very young.

My dog is an American Field Lab; she's smaller and much leaner than the English variety and built with a Ferrari engine. She enjoys exercise in all forms, but when she's not saving my life, which she's done several times, her passion is diving. Deep underwater. Like twelve feet down.

When no one had anything further to add about a possible plane crash, we moved on to more pressing business: drinking wine and catching up on Rose Avenue news.

"How's Jimmy settling in?" I asked Sally. "And how are you and Joe adapting to sharing your pastoral love nest with a relative?"

"Ha! No kin of mine is going to interfere with our horizontal hula. Thank God we put in that second story."

"Sally's cousin just moved here from Chicago," Peggy explained to Mary Ann. "He finally got some sense in him and left the freezing winters for a chilled margarita instead. Speaking of which, who needs a refill?"

Peggy was up and pouring the Gibbs Obsidian Block Reserve Cab I'd selected, particularly because of its bacon and black licorice tastes. You could put bacon in an old sneaker stew and I'd ask for seconds.

"We've got to get Jimmy together with Charlie. They already have the love of old planes in common," Sally said, receiving a heavy pour from Peggy.

"Maybe Peggy just wants to keep her new boyfriend to herself. How long has it been since you dated? Are these Castelvetrano olives?" Aimee's food vocabulary was expanding.

"The last man I dated was Vern, and I married him when I was twenty-one. Never you mind how long ago that was."

"I'm guessing it was when the best way to start your car was with a whip." That got me a punch in the arm from Peggy.

"Charlie's flying in today, I'll send him your way, Sally, and you can introduce him to Jimmy."

Out of the corner of my eye, I noticed Bardot, having been unsuccessful in drawing anyone away from their wine to play with her, had started tossing some of her sinkable toys into the pool.

She's got something up her furry sleeve . . .

When you enter my backyard with the pool, you'd think you'd landed in the Laki Lani Resort. It's a small tropical paradise with pink bougainvillea hanging over the water, birds of paradise and all colors of hibiscus lining the perimeter. Tiki masks hang from a covered patio area courtesy of me on a day of particularly enlightened procrastination from work.

I watched Mary Ann dial a number on her cell phone, listen and then disconnect, shaking her head.

"Something wrong?" Sally asked, launching into caregiver mode. (She's a former nurse.)

"It's probably nothing, but my husband, Jeb, left the house early this morning and I haven't heard from him since."

"Did you try calling one of his friends from work?" Peggy was now on the case.

"That's the thing, he just retired. And he was a chemist, so he mostly worked alone. These days he's always got some 'secret project' he's involved in. He's possibly been like this all along and I'm just now noticing it because I'm home more." Mary Ann seemed to be trying to convince herself of this.

Aimee's cell phone came to life with a ringtone playing Pharrell's "Happy."

"Hi honey! It's my boyfriend, Tom; he's working in the ER at St. John's Hospital," she stage-whispered to the group. "What? No! Oh my God, is he going to be okay?"

That got our undivided attention.

"Oh dear Lord, we'll be right over." She hung up and took a breath. "That *was* a plane crash you heard," Aimee said to Sally. "And Charlie was flying it. They just brought him into the hospital! He's awake and everything, which Tom says is a good sign. Charlie wanted Tom to pass along the news," Aimee assured Peggy.

Splash!

Bardot, having tried every trick in her playbook to get attention and failing, jumped into the pool with a belly flop that sent an airborne tsunami all over us.

"Halsey? Police," I heard a voice shout from the other side of the driveway gate. "We're coming in."

I watched as our local detective walked in, accompanied by two uniforms.

"Whatever it is this time, Augie, it will have to wait. We need to get to the hospital right away to be with Charlie," I said, noticing he was carrying a package sealed in a clear plastic evidence bag. Augie and I have a history together; I always seem to find trouble and he always attempts to pin it on me. Somehow, it all gets sorted out in the end.

"This package has a Rose Avenue address on it," Augie announced, showing it to the group. "Whose house number is this?"

Peggy shifted his arm to deflect the sun, so we could all get a good look.

"That's mine," Sally said. "What'd I get?" she asked, elated.

"Is crime so slow that you've taken to helping out the post office, Augie?" I couldn't resist.

"This package was removed from the plane Charlie was flying when it crashed on the runway," Augie said, ignoring my quip. I noticed the two cops were now flanking Sally.

Not a good sign.

Augie, dressed in a no-nonsense, dark gray suit, white shirt and maroon tie, always tried to give off that Secret Service, stoic tough-guy look but kept being betrayed by his accessories. Case in point: today his belt looked to be plain black leather, but when his jacket caught the wind, I could see the sides were canvas with embroidered sea marlin hooked and suspended in midair. His boxers also didn't perpetuate the myth. I'll explain. Augie's wardrobe has not quite caught up with his middle-aged belly, so his shirts often fan out between buttons. He has no butt and skinny legs, so he must need to hike up the undergarment above his belt to keep it in place. Today, I could make out *Calvin Klein* printed on the royal-blue-satin waistband.

Bardot, having retrieved her last toy from the pool's bottom, had come up for air. When she saw

Augie, someone she inexplicably adores, she raced out of the pool and ran toward him. She then remembered she needed to shake off the extra water and drenched his trousers.

There's going to be an extra treat in your bowl tonight, honey.

"Somebody get me a towel," Augie commanded. "As I was saying, this package was recovered from a large ice chest that was onboard, containing frozen fish. We opened it and found that it had a number of prescription drugs inside that appear to have originated in Mexico."

"I didn't order any medications from Mexico." Sally shook her head in disbelief. "Although I can see why people do; the prices here are getting ridiculous. Do you know how much my thyroid pills are? Thankfully, I'm on Joe's health plan from the university, which is excellent."

"I didn't know you had a thyroid problem. I wonder if I should get mine checked," Aimee mused.

"I heard eating asparagus was good for that," Mary Ann chimed in.

"*I wasn't finished,*" Augie yelled.

We stared at him like he'd sprouted horns. Even Bardot was taken aback and chose to watch the proceedings from a safe distance on a chaise lounge.

"When we examined one of the fish, we discovered heroin had been hidden inside it. A quick look at a few more fish revealed the same thing. We counted two dozen such 'heroin packages' total in the ice chest."

"What kind of fish were they?" I asked out of pure curiosity.

"It doesn't matter," Augie snapped at me. "So, Sally, I have no choice but to take you in for questioning."

"What?" Peggy shouted.

"We've all got to get to the ER. Tom says Charlie is awake and talking. He'll explain everything." Aimee held up her phone to Augie to somehow indicate proof of Tom's claim.

"Have you already talked to Charlie?" I asked Augie.

"No, he was in the ambulance when we arrived at the airport."

"Don't you think you should?" I could see his wheels turning in his head.

"All right, we'll go to the hospital. But you need to ride in the car with us, so I can keep an eye on you," Augie said, nodding at the cops to escort Sally.

"I knew it." We all looked at Sally and waited for her to say what *it* was.

"Knew what?" we asked in unison.

"With Charlie's accident, Jeb gone missing and my address on this package. The Curse of Rose Avenue is back!"

"Well, that's a relief. I was afraid it was something bad." Everyone looked at me, but no one was laughing.

As ERs go, the one at St. John's Hospital isn't so intimidating, although I wouldn't want to be there after ten p.m. on July 4. There was a separate entrance for ambulance deliveries, so we were only subject to the walking wounded. Today's assortment included a schoolgirl who'd clearly taken a face-plant when her cleats got caught during soccer practice. Her mom looked concerned, while the girl looked bored and unable to get Wi-Fi. In another area of the room, a family of about twelve had gathered, and it took me a moment to identify the patient. I narrowed it down to the oldest man in the group with the walker and labored breathing. This was a group that clearly ate away their worries; everyone was munching on something. A brother and sister had found a cart vendor that sold fresh fruit assortments and were digging into large clamshell servings. Foot-long subs were being passed around and inspected and smelled before being accepted by a family member. The only one not consuming was the old woman, who had to be ninety. Instead, she was playing a game on her iPad.

The woman at the front desk was being adamant about not letting the seven of us back to where Charlie was being treated. We settled for sending Peggy in first, while we hatched a plan for us to sneak in. Augie went with Peggy, and the cops continued to watch Sally. All that served to do was clean out a couple of guys who were seated in the waiting area and decided their boo-boos weren't bad enough to risk police attention. Their raw knuckles and swollen faces told enough of the story.

"I have no chance of getting in there with *Beavis*

and Butt-Head sticking to me like glue," Sally whispered to us just out of the cops' earshot. "You'll have to go in and report back what you saw."

"I don't need to go in either, I'm going to step outside and try Jeb again." Mary Ann headed for the door.

"There's Tom," Aimee said. "I'm going to walk in with him."

That left me, and because I didn't trust Augie to ask all the right questions, I wasn't about to miss a chance to talk to Charlie. I looked around the room hoping for inspiration. Beverly Baumgartner, RN, aka Nurse Ratched, at the desk, seemed to read my thoughts and was keeping a close eye on me.

You get more bees with honey, I heard my mom's voice say in my head.

"I'm going to get a water. You want anything?" I asked Sally loud enough for everyone to hear. She shook her head, looking dejected. That was all the impetus I needed to make my way to the gift shop.

When I returned, I sat back down and waited patiently. Sally looked at me, expecting more.

A few moments later, a delivery boy walked in with a half-dozen beautifully wrapped red roses. When he announced the name "Nurse Baumgartner" off the card, Nurse Ratched grew excited and signaled to him. That was my cue; I quietly slipped into the treatment area.

I found Peggy, Augie and Aimee standing outside one of the rooms. The curtain was drawn.

"He's getting x-rayed," Aimee explained.

I nodded. "How's he doing?"

"He's pretty banged up, but he's aware of everything going on and he's the same flirty Charlie that I've come to know and love. I'd be surprised if the nurses didn't file a class action suit." Peggy was using the light tone to steel her courage.

"You talk to him yet?" I asked Augie.

He shook his head. With every odd moan or sudden flurry of activity around us, he seemed to close more into himself. I started to suspect Augie wasn't a fan of sick people.

Good to know.

When they'd finally taken all the photos, blood samples, vitals and scans, we were allowed in to see Charlie.

"You always did know how to make an entrance," Peggy said, trying to tame some of his gray Irish curls. They'd first met, Sally once told me, when Peggy and her late husband, Vern, were newly married and enjoyed hosting poker night once a week with the guys from his job. That was short-lived, however, as Peggy would sit in and clean them out.

"Hey handsome, you up for telling us what happened?" I asked, noticing that Augie had his eyes firmly fixed on his shoes, I'm guessing to avoid seeing the IV needle in Charlie's arm.

Needles. Augie's Achilles' heel . . .

"I landed, same as always, it's a clear, picture-perfect day so no problems whatsoever. But then, once I hit the tarmac, I felt the plane's wheels run over something and I skidded. I tried to correct for it but lost control and crashed into the hangar. Thankfully, the plane had slowed considerably by then. It could have been a lot worse, but this one's not getting away that easily." He gave Peggy a warm smile.

Peggy, in return, spooned some ice chips into his dry mouth.

"Are you sure about hitting something? Could it actually have been a malfunction with the wheels or engine?" Augie asked, still not looking at him. "Because when I arrived on the scene, the runway was clear."

"I'm positive. There was no mechanical or pilot error!" Charlie was getting worked up.

"Of course there wasn't," I said, "and you're the best one to know, Charlie. Was anyone from the ground crew there who could help clear this up?"

"That's the thing. I found out that the regular guy, Rusty, went home sick earlier that morning. Food poisoning or something."

Food poisoning is the classic excuse for playing hooky, I thought to myself. You could always claim it was a twenty-four-hour thing and be back at work the next day.

"It could have been some sort of critter you hit, and it was well enough to crawl away somewhere. The bones will turn up once the hawks are done with it," Peggy concluded.

"What can you tell us about the cargo you were transporting?" Augie was now pretending to study a poster on the wall illustrating the Heimlich maneuver.

"It was a total last-minute thing. When I checked in at Montgomery Airport in San Diego, there was a note waiting for me asking if I could fly a cooler of seafood to Santa Monica. Someone would pick it up there. I was going through my flight check and had almost forgotten about it when a guy in a golf cart drove up with it."

"Did you know this guy?" I asked.

"No, and I hardly looked at him. It was time to go. I've done some back-and-forth deliveries in the past; everybody does. What's so important about this one?"

"Tell him, Augie." This time I physically turned Augie to face him, and he turned sheet white.

What? Augie needed to see Charlie's reaction.

As I expected, Charlie was shocked to learn he'd been flying illegal prescription drugs and narcotics from point A to point B. He insisted he knew nothing more than that the ice chest contained frozen fish.

"I never even looked inside it. The guy—he was dressed like a waiter or something—loaded it in the back himself. Am I in some kind of police trouble?"

Peggy got indignant. "He'd better not be. You've got nothing, Augie."

Augie stared into space and thought for a moment. It was just enough time for me to snoop in one of the supply drawers in the room to find what I needed.

"At the moment, I have no reason not to believe you, Charlie. You said you didn't see or know what was in the ice chest. This investigation is just starting. I'll be in touch if I have any more questions." Augie turned his back on us, hoping to make a hasty retreat.

"Then the same needs to go for Sally," I argued. He looked at me, and horror struck his face. It could have been because I was using a plastic-wrapped syringe to make my point.

"Yes," he meekly replied, looking at the wall. "I'll take my guys and she is free to go. For now."

"Thank God," Aimee said.

CHAPTER 2

Spitfire Grill is the local eatery, draft-beer pur-
veyor and wine-tasting venue located at the
Santa Monica airport just next to the Museum of
Flying. Sally and I were on our way there from the
ER to meet her cousin Jimmy and her husband Joe
for dinner. Despite the curse Sally had declared,
some good news came out of the day: Jimmy got a
part-time job working at the museum as a docent.
When he'd called and told Sally, her mood immediately picked up.

"So, I've got to ask, you were the one who had
the flowers sent to that Nurse Baumgartner in the
ER, correct?"

I gave her my best innocent-puppy look.

"Oh, come on, and what did the note that came
with the roses say?"

"It said *You're doing a heckuva job!* Not that I know
firsthand . . ."

Sally gave a hearty laugh as we pulled into the parking lot.

The Grill has everything a diner could want: cozy booths, kitsch and lots of local aviation history mounted on the walls. The menu is suited both for someone with a wicked hangover and a healthy-eating-conscious, exercise fanatic. If you know any of those; I don't.

Jimmy and Joe were already seated in a booth when we arrived, taking gulps of what looked like Guinness Stout. Jimmy is tall, like his cousin Sally, but not nearly as lean and toned. Too much Chicago deep-dish pizza perhaps.

Sally's husband, Joe, is quite an entity on to himself. Whereas Sally will tell you what's on her mind and do so in a way that forces you to sit up and take notice, Joe is more like the one pale yellow tulip on a hillside of showy reds. You may not notice the flower at first, but when you do, you're fascinated by how it quietly stands out and dying to find out its story. He is an elegant black man, always dressed to the scholarly nines. Joe earns his living as a tenured philosophy professor at UCLA and watches and listens deeply to everything around him. In some ways, he is the quintessential voyeur, and I love hearing his observations.

I launched into recounting the twisted events of the day, the package and the drugs. Our server, seeing that we were deep in conversation, quietly left menus and gave us some time. When I finished, it was Jimmy who reacted first.

"That's the dumbest thing I've ever heard a cop

try to pull, and I must remind you that I come from Chicago!"

"Right?" Sally said, making a circle with her index finger along the side of her head. "There's a village around here missing its idiot. Oh great, I'm starving. Remind me of your name again, dear?" Sally said as our waitress approached.

"Of course, I'm Britt. I've only been here a couple of months, so I don't expect people to remember me yet."

"Well, I certainly will," Jimmy said, admiring her long chestnut hair and Cupid's bow smile.

"This is my cousin Jimmy. Never mind him, he's actually harmless. And the handsome man sitting across from me is my husband, Joe."

"A pleasure to meet you. What brings you to Spitfire, Britt? Do you have aspirations to take to the sky?" Joe asked, subtly digging, which gave me an idea.

"What? No, the side of my brain that works on math and physics suffers from arrested development, I'm afraid." She looked at me and smiled again.

"Hi Britt, I'm Halsey, and contrary to popular belief I am not part of this beautiful family. I am a close friend and neighbor."

That got a laugh out of her, and I continued. "You may not become a pilot, but I'll bet you know everything that's going on with them since working here? Got any good stories? We've been known to reward juicy tidbits with refreshment in the form of fine wines."

She got down on her haunches at the head of

the table, excited by the conspiratorial challenge I'd laid down.

"Girl, you have no idea. Some of these guys around here think they're God. You should hear the bragging and boasting that goes on, especially during happy hour."

"You need to come to our wine club meetings; we're just over on Rose Avenue. Here, write down your cell number and I'll call you with the specifics," Sally told her.

"Thank you, but I don't always know my work schedule until the last minute," Britt apologized.

"Honey, we meet once a week, sometimes more; you'll come when you can and spill all the salacious details about these airmen."

"Did you hear or see the plane that crashed today?" I took over from Sally, who seemed to have forgotten she was a drug-dealing suspect.

"No, I worked breakfast and had just left. But I heard the pilot's going to be okay."

"We just came from seeing him in the ER, and yes, thankfully, it's nothing serious. Charlie said his plane hit something on the runway, but when it was inspected, there was no sign of any obstruction. You hear any chatter in here tonight about that? The police claim there were drugs hidden in the cargo of the plane." I looked around, trying to pick out the pilots.

"Not so far, but I'll keep my ears open. You all know what you want? I just tasted the chicken pot pie special in the kitchen and it's delish!"

We gave Britt our orders. I'd studied the salads and then opted for the Flying Tiger Burger with bacon, cheddar, and BBQ sauce.

May I remind you that I've had nothing to eat since Wine Club?

When Britt returned with our drinks, I thought I'd give it one more shot.

"Hey Britt, you must know the ground crew that works at the airport. We'd heard Rusty went home sick this morning. You know who would've taken his place when our friend Charlie landed?"

She gave a dry laugh. "Rusty, he's something special that guy. He's got the temperament of a wild hog. I've seen him get cranky just because it's Tuesday."

"He's a real charmer," Sally jumped in. "Does he ever get into arguments or quarrels with the pilots?"

"Not that I know of; he's more angry at life itself. But you should ask Jonas, his young apprentice. In fact, he probably took over the landings when Rusty claimed he was sick."

She said "claimed," I noticed.

"I just met the kid," Jimmy announced. "He said he was working late tonight. I'll take you over to the museum after dinner and you all can have a talk. I've got to pick up my ID tag anyway," he said, puffing with pride.

There was no mistaking that Sally and Jimmy were related. Both proudly sported winter-white hair that gave haloes to their faces. Jimmy also had the same aquiline nose and smooth skin, but the dark circles under his eyes told me that he'd had his share of burdens over the years. I hoped the sun and slower pace of Mar Vista would melt those away.

By the time our plates were cleaned and the last

drops of wine were drunk, I could see a weight had been lifted from Sally's shoulders. I suspected she'd thought, as I had hoped, that this whole thing with Augie would blow over quickly.

We paid our bill and reminded Britt on the way out that we'd be calling her for Wine Club.

"I can't wait. You're my first friends since I moved up here from San Diego!"

I pushed the swinging door and felt resistance from the other side. I tried again, and the same thing. I decided to let whoever was on the outside come on in first. It was Mary Ann's husband, Jeb, and he looked disoriented and out of sorts. We helped him to a stool at the bar.

"May we have some water for him, please?" Sally asked the bartender. "Let me feel your forehead. Can you tell me what happened, honey?"

Jeb took a careful couple of sips of water before saying anything. For a big man, he looked awfully sunken and frail. If someone asked, I'd describe Jeb as tall and jolly, likely to burst into song if the mood struck him. Tonight, he looked like a zombie whose spirit had left him.

"It's the craziest thing," he finally said. "I'd driven up to the airport and parked by the observation deck this morning, the sun was out, and I thought I'd watch the planes for a while. I woke up in my car just a little bit ago and I have no idea what happened between the time I parked until now."

"I'm calling Mary Ann. Joe, can you drive Jeb home?" I asked. I watched as Jeb, suddenly very thirsty, drained his glass and signaled to the bartender for a refill.

"Sure can, or should I take him directly to the ER?" Joe asked, examining Jeb with a concerned eye.

"Good God no. At this hour it'll be a zoo," Sally replied continuing her examination of him. "He's dehydrated, but his pulse is settling down now. Halsey, tell Mary Ann that if he gets any worse, she should take him to urgent care in the Marina. But I think he'll be okay."

I relayed the message, and we all helped him to Joe's car.

"I feel much better already," Jeb said, climbing in. "It's just so foolish that I can't remember what happened."

"It'll all come back to you, don't you worry, honey," Sally soothed.

We watched Joe and Jeb drive off.

"That was kind of strange, wasn't it?" Jimmy asked as we traversed the lawn to the museum next door.

"I'd skip the qualifier, Jimmy. Plain and simple, Jeb was acting very odd."

"I wonder what meds he's on," Sally mused. "They may need to be tweaked."

We followed Jimmy around the back of the building to the staff entrance. Instead of entering the museum, Jimmy turned right and unlocked another door that led into an adjacent hangar, where the plane restoration was done. The only light in the place was coming from the far end of the building.

"Jonas? It's Jimmy, the new guy you met this afternoon. It's late; shouldn't you be knocking off soon?" he said loudly.

We heard no response.

"I'll bet he's in the flight simulator back there," Jimmy said to us, heading in that direction. "He was telling me today how he couldn't wait to get his pilot's license so he could take off whenever he wanted."

Our footsteps echoed in the dark cavern as Sally and I followed closely behind Jimmy. Darkness can make a lot of places creepy, but the shadows and partially illuminated propellers, wings and wheels of these old planes made me think I was being surrounded by decomposing dinosaurs. I finally relaxed when we reached the simulator capsule, but that was very short-lived.

"Ladies first," Jimmy said, and I climbed the metal steps to the cockpit entrance. Once my eyes adjusted to the light inside, I could take in the gruesome scene and felt bile rise into my throat.

"Sweet Jesus!" Sally screamed when she stuck her head in, followed by a deep groan from Jimmy after he did the same.

Sitting at the controls was a body I assumed was Jonas. It was slumped over, and I could see a trail of white foam had escaped his cracked lips. This told me that his demise had been recent. There was no question Jonas was dead, and given what I'd seen, he was certainly better off.

CHAPTER 3

Thankfully, the police department had a whole new crew on at this time of night, so we escaped the wrath and chastisement of Augie. The detective and officers approached the scene and us matter-of-factly, giving no indication we were anything more than innocent discoverers. We were questioned individually, and I was the last to go.

"Ms. Hall, why don't you tell me what brought you to the hangar at this time of night," the detective asked me as we talked outside the building. He had my driver's license in hand and I guessed was running a check as we spoke. If I'm being exceedingly generous, he was tall, dark, and handsome. But in a cartoony, Dick Tracy way.

"As I explained to the other two officers, I was accompanying my friend, Sally, and her cousin to the museum. Jimmy had just been hired to do some docent work for them, and he wanted to pick up his new ID card. We'd come from dinner at Spitfire."

I left out the part about looking for Jonas to ask about the crash and Rusty. That would add nothing to the investigation except get us in hot water and keep us here longer. Luckily, I had managed to tell Sally and Jimmy to do the same before they separated us.

"Wouldn't the tags have been in the museum office? What brought you into the restoration hangar?"

"Jimmy. He was bursting with pride at getting this job, and he wanted to give us the grand tour. He's going through a major life change at the moment. He and his wife of thirty-two years recently got divorced, his kids are all grown and the only thing that kept him stuck in Chicago was the ice and snow. He moved out here a month ago and is just starting to get his footing."

"Were you supposed to be meeting anyone in here?"

"Who? No."

The detective was writing furiously in his notepad, and I instantly regretted giving him so much detail about Jimmy, harmless as it seemed.

"Okay, I understand a peek into the place, but what drew you to walk all the way to the other end of the hangar to the flight simulator?"

I had to be careful now.

"There was a light left on in the simulator. Jimmy wanted to turn it off."

He stared me in the eye for a minute.

"No other reason?"

"What other reason are you looking for?"

Oops. Now he was getting mad.

"Who found the body?" he asked, ignoring my question.

"I did. I was the first one up the steps." I felt the blood leave my face, remembering. "It was, is, the worst thing I've ever seen."

"Did you know the victim?"

"No."

"How long have you known Jimmy?"

"Just about a month, since he moved here."

"He's never visited before? Did your friend Sally over there talk about him much?"

"No and not really." It was time to give terse, vanilla responses until I knew where he was going with this.

"One last question, Ms. Hall. Did Jimmy tell you that he'd known the victim Jonas was working late and he wanted to check on him?"

Rats. Jimmy must have forgotten my directive. This cat was now caught way out on the limb of a very tall tree.

I opened my mouth, not knowing what would come out.

"Detective?" We were interrupted by one of the officers. "Something you need to see."

He gave me a slight grin, knowing he'd caught me and I was going to sweat it out for a bit longer. He flattened his hand and held his palm out to me, indicating I was to stay put. He followed the officer back inside.

Just like Bardot, I obeyed until he was gone and then snuck over to the hangar entrance to eavesdrop.

"We ran this guy's license through Chicago PD.

It's expired now, but he has an outstanding moving violation and some parking tickets he's ducked. Enough to bring him in?"

The detective nodded and caught sight of me at the door.

"There was some large animal stalking me! How could you leave me alone out there in the dark to be shredded by some rabid coyote? With distemper!"

Not sure why I added that last affliction.

"Let's read Jimmy his rights and take him to the station," he told the officer.

The detective looked back at me.

"You didn't answer my last question."

"And now I'm not going to. You want to read me my rights and take me in too?" I stuck out my chin and cocked my head.

"I'll be in touch," he said, walking away.

I stuck my head into the hangar.

"How will I ever sleep until you do? I'm so excited I could just die."

Who knew that my words, bad choices as they were, would be amplified and echo throughout the structure.

I dropped Sally back at home and could see she was completely spent after the day's roller-coaster of emotions. I tried to assure her that all would be settled in the morning, but I didn't sound convincing, so how could I expect her to have faith? She reiterated that the curse was back.

When I pulled into my driveway, I was greeted first by a happy, furry, yellow face peering out the dining room window and secondly by the diminutive Latina from next door. Her face was framed by blue-black, dyed chin-length hair betrayed by a band of gray at the crown. She was thin and looked a bit frail. Until she opened her mouth.

"What were you doing out so late? You bring me something from Spitfire?"

That's Marisol, my nosy, strangely clairvoyant neighbor who has been both the bane of my existence and my lifesaver since I moved to Rose Avenue.

"How'd you know I was at Spitfire?" I asked, getting out of the car with the carryout bag. I'd put in the order for Marisol's favorite when we went to the museum and Britt had been kind enough to keep it warm for me. She'd left by the time I retrieved it.

As I said, Marisol seems to know things without being there, without getting reports from witnesses or by any other earthly means. I'm not saying she's some sort of mystical spirit, although there have been times when I've wished I could load her on her broomstick and send her to the moon.

"That sure smells like a turkey burger," she said, taking the bag. Her eyes lit up like sparklers when she peeked inside the container. She took a sniff and grinned wide enough for the moonlight to catch her gold tooth and illuminate her face.

If only I were so easy to please.

"Go grab Bardie; she's been locked up for hours. We'll eat on my back patio."

I dug my keys out of my purse, and when I looked

up a few seconds later, she was gone. She's also famous for her disappearing acts.

When Bardot and I entered her backyard through the driveway, she'd already eaten a good chunk of her burger with such gusto, she hadn't bothered to stop and do anything about the ketchup dripping from the corners of her mouth and her chin.

"When was the last time you ate?" I asked, watching her Hoover some fries.

"Around six. Here Bardie," she said, pointing to the one fry that had gotten away and was making a run for it on the cobblestone.

"Marisol, what have I told you about calling my dog by her real name?"

"I dunno."

"Yes, you do. Her name is Bardot, after the French actress and swimsuit model Brigitte Bardot. Not Bardie, Bard, Borrow or any other derivatives. You understand that, right?"

Her eyes grew wide and her legs swung in the lawn chair hanging about a half foot from the ground. She looked like a child being scolded. That was until she finished her last bite of burger, dispensed with the pickle and let out a burp that seemed to emanate from her coccyx.

Bardot's head went up in the air; she took in a noseful and licked her lips as if she'd just walked into an aged steak house. I figured out which way the wind was blowing and moved alee. When the air had cleared enough to breathe, I filled her in on the crash and the events after, including the murder. She listened, but her expression never changed. Even after I told her how I found Jonas.

I'd seen her be stoic like this before and I never knew if it was due to fear, boredom or some kind of defense mechanism she'd designed to brace herself against bad news.

"Now Jimmy's a suspect and Sally's worried sick. I've got to figure out a way to help them. We need to find out who sent that cooler of fish in the first place; that'll be a start. I just wish I'd had a chance to look at the fish to see what kind they were. That would at least tell us if they were local or not."

"Who's got 'em now, can't you ask them?"

"Augie. I'm not exactly his favorite person in the world . . . but you are his favorite aunt!" I said, remembering. "Please talk to him? I just need to know the species."

"I'll think about it, because you gave me the burger and all."

"That's mighty big of you."

I noticed a slight grin cross her face, telling me that I'd get my answer one way or another. We have a funny relationship, the two of us. We freely throw insults back and forth but seldom admit to the true affection we have for each other.

"You must have seen your share of plane crashes at the airport, given all the years you've lived here, Marisol."

"You bet I seen 'em. Taking off at one end and landing at the other is the most common. But I've also seen planes sticking nose first into people's house roofs."

I felt my face blanch.

"Don't worry; Rose Avenue is parallel to the airport, so it's difficult to hit. I'm not saying it couldn't happen." She crossed herself, looked to the sky, then to the grass and finally plucked out a clover from her lawn and pulled off its leaves one by one.

I half-expected it to start raining.

"Have you ever heard of anyone being murdered at the airport?"

"How would I know a thing like that?"

"Because you're a snoop. You know everything."

"I am not!" My accusation got her to hop down off her chair to proclaim her innocence.

"Be careful. I don't want you to fall and break your neck. Well . . ."

She gave me the death stare.

"I'm just kidding. So, no murders, huh?"

"Back in the day, there were fistfights, but the only people killed were riding in those tin cans in the sky."

It was getting late and I was getting nowhere.

"How much do you know about Jeb and Mary Ann?" I asked, switching gears. That whole scene with Jeb was still bothering me.

"They're nice, quiet neighbors."

Meaning she's spied on them and found nothing.

"Except lately."

I sat down on a log that bordered the lawn and pulled Bardot into me for warmth. Marisol loved to drag out her stories when she had something I wanted.

"Go on."

"A couple of weeks ago I seen Jeb walking back and forth on the sidewalk in front of his house, really early in the morning."

"Do you ever sleep? Never mind, please continue."

"It turns out he was waiting for the mail carrier.

When she approached, Jeb stopped her on the sidewalk and they had a conversation. She then handed him a package and put the rest of their mail through the slot."

"What did the package look like? Big, small, a box?"

"It looked like a package!"

"Marisol, your powers of observation rival a hungry hawk's."

"Okay, it was about the size of a shoebox, tan paper and only a little bit poofed out."

"You mean filled. You're talking about how thick the package was?"

"I mean poofed out. Is all that wine drinking making your hearing go bad?"

I exhaled to control my rising temper.

"What did Jeb do with the package?"

"He put it in the trunk of his car."

"Is that it?"

"Yes."

I stood up to go.

"Except . . ."

"Except what?"

"Except I saw him do it again, wait outside for the mail carrier. But she didn't have no package for him."

"When did this happen?"

"This morning."

My head was exploding, and it was time to tuck into bed with my dog and a rich glass of Italian Valpolicella.

"Oh, I almost forgot. Was there ever something called 'the Curse of Rose Avenue'?"

"I don't know what you're talking about. First your hearing goes, and now your brain."

She disappeared into her house. I couldn't help but think her denial of knowing about a curse was a sure sign the opposite was true.

CHAPTER 4

The next day arrived with another cloudless sky to warm my now pathetically low body threshold for cold temperatures. Less than forty degrees is simply inhuman. Thankfully, you could count those days on one hand. Funny how, for a place with consistently lovely weather, we pay such close attention to the forecast each day. I'd become an admirer of nuances, and today's weather dictated that it was time to climb a mountain. The first order of business was to prepare a picnic.

As I do every morning, I went out and surveyed the back forty to see which crops were ready for picking. Okay, so it's actually an eight-foot-by-five-foot raised bed, but it has proved bountiful. Just not so much today. My garden yielded a couple of nice-looking green onions, but that was it.

"Time to go up the hill to our garden plot, Bardot." She cocked her head and gave me her trademark ear-to-ear smile. Bardot then ran inside and to the front door, where she showed her excitement with a series of leaps off her back legs that thrust her higher and higher in the air with each jump. When she saw me turn instead and go into my bedroom, she let out a whimper.

"What? I can't go out in tiny pajama shorts and a tank top. You may be able to walk around in the nude, but in these parts, they don't appreciate humans going out half naked." Her indifference told me that she wasn't buying it, and when I remembered we lived just a few miles from Venice Beach, I understood why.

I changed into my hiking outfit for the day: army green shorts with lots of pockets, an off-shoulder white embroidered peasant blouse and pink high-top Chuck Taylors. I have to keep up appearances, after all. I put a leash on Bardot and we went out the door and started up the hill.

I live toward the top end of our section of Rose Avenue, which allows for an unobstructed ocean breeze that cools the house all year long. At the very top of the hill sits a community garden offering six acres of fifteen-by-fifteen-foot plots of incredibly rich soil available for rent and almost guaranteed to produce, well, produce. I use the term *available for rent* loosely, as this is some of the most coveted land in Los Angeles and is willed down through families for generations.

So how did a city girl like me end up with a plot on the hill? The wonderful girls in the Rose Avenue Wine Club gave it to me last year for my birthday. It had become available in a nasty probate battle and they were at the right place at the right time. How could they have known that the octogenarian at the center of the fight had been buried alive in said plot? Of course, I—rather Bardot—uncovered the body, and it all turned into a very long story. But that's a present for another Christmas.

We reached the top and found my little garden. The view up there was fabulous and the briny air I breathed in while admiring the ocean on the horizon made me think of Blue Hawaii drinks and bronzed Hawaiian men.

Don't judge me.

To my delight, a garden buddy had left me a basket of apricots from her overabundant crop. I clipped some watercress and arugula from my little horn of plenty and lunch was starting to take shape in my mind. I needed one more ingredient to complete this gastronomic palette. A grapefruit for the dressing. The owner of the tree near my plot had given me carte blanche to help myself, with the subtext that I would partake modestly. When I examined the branches, I saw that for the most part they were bare. Except for one large almost-bursting-with-flavor fruit at the top. It clearly needed to be liberated.

"Bardot, if I fall and break my leg, go and get Marisol for help. If I fall and break my neck, go and get the bottle of La Tâche I've been saving for Armageddon."

I hoisted myself up onto the first branch and looked skyward into the tree to chart my course. These trees are typically wider than they are tall, and the younger ones have relatively small, wispy appendages. This particular beauty was probably over one hundred years old, and a proud specimen indeed.

As I snaked through the branches, I looked down and saw Bardot waiting patiently for me to send a squirrel her way. The glass is always half full for her. When I reached my quarry I still had to stretch another foot or so to get my hand on the fruit. When I did, balancing on my tiptoes, I yanked, but the grapefruit remained firmly attached to the limb. I was a good twenty feet above the ground and was not about to climb down, trod home and return with some pruning shears. No, I was going to give it the good old Halsey try.

I could clearly see the Santa Monica airport from here, brimming with activity as small planes taxied, took off or landed. The sound of their engines buzzing echoed up the hill.

Time for my second attempt.

I elongated my body and caught hold of the fruit. My other hand was clasped around the strong center trunk to hold me steady. This time when I pulled, I lifted my feet to let the entire weight of my body apply the pressure. Two things happened next and I'm not sure in which order: The grapefruit broke free from its stem and a yellow and black small plane buzzed by only about fifteen feet from my head.

For every action, there is an equal and opposite reaction.

My feet never found the branch again; the hand holding on to the trunk slipped, and because I stupidly refused to let go of the prize in the other hand, I was now falling through the tree. I would like to attribute the next occurrence to my catlike reflexes, but in truth, it was only because I was afraid of landing on Bardot and killing her.

My free arm caught a horizontal branch and I was able to swing and wrap my legs around it like a monkey would. My other hand hung freely, gripping the grapefruit. I got my bearings and assessed my situation. I was about six feet from the ground, Bardot was jumping up and down and wagging her tail and one of my neighbors and her two young kids had stopped their nature walk to view what they knew would be far more interesting to their social media audiences. The kids had their cell phones out and were snapping away.

"Oh my goodness, how can we help?" asked the mom warily.

It's not every day you see someone risk their life for a grapefruit that can easily be purchased a mile away at Whole Foods.

"There's a ladder over by the fence. Can you bring it here and open it?"

"Sean?"

"On it!" The boy went on his mission like an exemplary first responder.

When at last I was on terra firma, I took a breath and surveyed the damage. I had some scrapes on my forearm and a skinned shin. And an intact grapefruit.

"Thank you, guys, so much, I don't know what I would have done if you hadn't been walking by. Bardot is a wonderful dog, but I've never been able to get her to set up a ladder for me. She always grumbles something about opposable thumbs."

The kids giggled.

"Did you see that plane? It nearly hit me!"

"I've seen them lose altitude on their approach to the airport for landing, but never that low," Mom said, nodding to her offspring as if this was a teachable moment. "Are you sure you're okay? I can go get the car and drive you home."

"Thank you, that's sweet. But no motor vehicle is going to relieve what hurts the most right now." I too can play teacher, and the kids were hoping I'd reveal some huge gouge on my body spewing entrails.

"My pride." I laughed. "This ranks right up there as one of my silliest ideas."

Mom gave me an appreciative smile and class was dismissed. As they continued their walk, I heard Sean say, "That *was* pretty dumb."

An hour later, Bardot and I were on our way to the Santa Monica Mountains. The Pacific Coast Highway is more of a scenic coastal throwback road than it is an asphalt speedway. It hugs the curves and bends of the hills on one side and the shoreline on the other. Along the way, you'll pass real estate offices, fresh seafood shacks where you dine al fresco on picnic tables and about every mile a place where you can rent kayaks, surfboards and bikes. And, because we are heading through Malibu, there are also the prerequisite yoga studios, cashmere retailers and tattoo removal services. Once Bardot got her bearings and a whiff of briny critters, she was beside herself with excitement. Her squeals and barks ebbed and flowed like the sounds a kid makes on a roller coaster.

"You know where you're going, don't you?" I peeked at her behind the safety gate of my SUV.

That solicited a high-pitched yip that made my ears ring like a dinner bell. My cell phone rang, and I engaged the Bluetooth on my dash. Speak of the devil.

"Hi honey, we're about ten minutes out."

"Wonderful," Jack said. "I've got one more set of drills to run and then we can get lunch somewhere down at the beach."

"We're bringing lunch and you'll never believe what I went through to get it."

"I'm afraid to ask . . ."

"You don't have to. There'll be visual cues."

"Okay, knowing you, now I'm really curious."

We turned off PCH and started climbing a canyon road up the mountain. This was one of the first things that drew me to California, the fact that you could hike steep terrain in the morning and cool off in the ocean in the afternoon. And still be home in time for cocktail hour. Or Wine Club.

My amber-eyed boo, Jack, lives up to his name. He's an excellent nonaggressive/reward motivation dog trainer, although since I've known him, cats, llamas and a barn owl have also benefitted from his tutelage. He's a member of CARA, the Canine Rescue Association that uses canine/handler teams to perform search-and-rescue missions saving people in all kinds of bad situations. He's on call 24/7 and is also one of the lead instructors for training new teams. And if those trades weren't enough, Jack is also a pilot specializing in helicopters and works with his friend Mark from the DEA from time to time, using dogs to help them make drug busts.

Knowing all this and taking in his six-four frame, you would think this guy spends his free time watching monster trucks and drinking hard lemonade. Nothing could be further from the truth. His dad died tragically when he was a boy and he was raised by a group of women who nurtured his sensitive and artistic side.

Too good to be true?

He's the real deal, and I'm the one with the flaws of a G/SI1 diamond. But I'm working on it; he's a keeper and I just need to get there.

The road narrowed and changed to dirt as we approached the base level where the training and hikes start out. The hillsides were lush green from all the rain we had in January, and the scent in the air had changed from warm saline to a rich coniferous breeze. We parked at the far end of the clearing to give a wide berth to the training vehicles. I wasn't exactly sure what Jack had in mind today, but Bardot and I have a reputation for totally disrupting his exercises with unintended, profoundly embarrassing stunts. Not always well received in a situation where people and dogs are learning to save lives.

"Bardot, we are going to behave like wallpaper today and completely fade into the forest background. We will do nothing to make people notice us, laugh at us or hate us more than they already do. Capisce?"

She had sat and was looking at me intently, for Jack's benefit, no doubt. To him, she was the poster girl for doggy obedience. For me, not so much. We walked over to the periphery of the circle of teams that had formed around Jack. He no-

ticed and waved to us, prompting Bardot to immediately drop into a down stay.

"Gooood girl," he rewarded her.

"Nobody likes a brownnoser," I whispered to
her before realizing how ludicrous a statement
that was to make to a dog.

"Today is about specialized scent training," Jack
told the group. "It isn't enough for your dog to
track just any item with a human scent; you need
to focus on the victim that needs rescuing. Most
times this will happen in places where lots of people have walked or hiked over the years and inad-
vertently dropped things. If we are lucky enough
to have an item of clothing, say with the victim's
odor on it, we'll save a lot of time and avoid dead
ends."

People—okay, the women—looked at Jack with
a combination of admiration and lust. His warm,
amber, almond-shaped eyes drew you in, and his
neatly trimmed beard and shaved head completed
the gentle giant look.

*Better check and repair my makeup; nothing in life is
a sure thing.*

"For today's exercise, I have had my team plant
some trigger items around a half-mile perimeter
of the forest entrance. You'll see flag markers
where the scene ends. There are some twenty bits
of clothing, maps, water bottles and food items out
there, ten of which have my scent on them. I'm
going to pass around pieces of cloth that I have
handled for you to use to track. If your dog starts
to get distracted or confused, use this to refocus.
The goal is to locate one of the items I've touched
and bring it back here. Any questions?"

All the women raised their hands, of course. They had the kind of know-it-all, show-off questions that always began with *Isn't it true that . . .*

I was about to make a snide comment to Bardot when I noticed she was gone.

I must have dropped her leash while I was applying a shimmering coat of Summer Breeze whipped matte lipstick. I knew I needed to find her before the rescue teams descended, so while Jack was fielding offers I slipped into the forest.

"Bardot?" I softly whispered. I saw a flash of yellow race past me that was either my dog or a doe trying to escape a particularly concupiscent buck.

What's the difference between beer nuts and deer nuts? Beer nuts are over five dollars and deer nuts are just under a buck.

I saw branches move and heard rustling coming from about three o'clock from my position and headed in that direction.

"Bardot! Come!"

Nothing.

"I'm holding a perfectly seasoned, medium-rare filet mignon in my hands smothered in black truffle butter . . ."

That did the trick; I saw her head pop up. I have always marveled at her ability to hold five tennis balls in her mouth at once. Right now, she must have almost twice as many items locked between her canine canines.

"Get over here right now!"

She turned tail and took off with me in pursuit. But I couldn't match her speed or ability to jump over or duck under tree branches. I lost sight of her just before doing a face-plant into a perfectly placed mud puddle. Realizing my predicament and what I must look like, I decided to lay low until, say, the Fourth of July, when I hoped people would be otherwise distracted.

"Halsey? You in there, babe?"

I tried to become one of those rain forest denizens who can morph into their environment with pigmentation manipulation.

"I see you, Halsey. Are you hurt?"

My cover, or lack thereof, was blown, and I had no choice.

"Coming."

I did what I could with my hair and lipstick, but I knew the result would still be disconcerting unless you were an überfan of *Naked and Afraid*.

When I emerged into the clearing, I was dismayed to see that the rescue teams had not yet been released to the hunt and still stood in a love circle around Jack. Beside him sat Bardot, and I counted eight items she'd laid at his feet.

"I'm glad I stopped her before she ruined the entire exercise. Jack, shouldn't they all be on their way to find the triggers?"

I tried to sound cheery and nonchalant. Jack looked at me and rubbed his chin. I smiled at him and he repeated the action, this time more deliberately. I looked at the group to see if they were doing the same, thinking this was perhaps a new hand signal for the dogs. They hadn't moved. When Jack repeated the movement a third time, I slowly raised my hand to my chin. What came off into my palm was a brown, sticky clump of something surrounded by pine needles and wood chips.

I didn't need to get my nose any closer to my hand to pick up its foul odor.

"What Bardot picked up in there can't possibly be all the ones with your scent on them, can they?" I gave him a cocked-headed, incredulous look.

He nodded back to me that they were.

"That's just crazy. I'll go back to my car now, clean up a little. Sorry."

I shrunk away and heard Jack tell Bardot to follow me.

"Bardot, if I didn't know that English is your first language, I could accept that you had trouble understanding me when I said we were to remain inconspicuous today. But you heard me and Jack's instructions to the group and just decided to steal the show, didn't you?"

I couldn't disguise my pride and she knew it. We reached the car and I gave her water and did triage on myself. I opened the back and Bardot hopped up, happy and ready for a nap. I sat down beside her to wallow in shame for today's buffoonery.

"Are we having a tailgate party? Cool!" Jack said, giving me a kiss on the cheek.

I pulled away. "Are you crazy? You could catch swine flu or mad deer disease from me!"

He laughed. "It looks like you did a pretty good job of washing your face."

"Yeah, well, I also did a pretty good job of ruining your training session and wasting those volunteers' time."

"I think that honor goes to Bardot. Did you tell her to go find those items?"

"No, of course not. She decided to do that all on her own."

"Well, at least one of you listens to me. Hey, Bardot raised the bar for those teams, and I'll bet they'll be practicing every day until our next session. Did you get that scrape on your arm from chasing after her in the woods?"

I looked at the two-inch-wide, arrow-shaped abrasion across my upper arm that in the military would mean I was a corporal.

"No, I got this falling down a tree when an airplane buzzed by above my head."

"Fine, don't tell me."

"I just did!" I was getting cranky.

"Why don't we spread the blanket down on the grass and you can tell me all about it over lunch?" Jack said, unloading the goodies from my car.

We dined on chicken salad with arugula and a grapefruit vinaigrette on crusty pieces of baguette and had cold poached apricots and Stilton for dessert. We each had a glass of Hanna Winery Sauvignon Blanc that calmed me down enough to tell my tree story without yelling or crying.

"Geez, I don't suppose you got the tail numbers?"

"Jack, I was clinging to a branch for dear life. Does this thing happen often? Do planes need to get that low before landing at the airport?"

"No way, never. There are strict rules about the approach, and even if someone ignored them, they wouldn't be flying low over that location south of the runway."

"You think this was done on purpose?" My voice had gone up an octave.

"I know it sounds crazy. I mean, who would do such a thing?"

It was time to fill Jack in on last night's dead-body discovery and Charlie's events leading up to the hit. This time he shook his head, not because he was incredulous but because I had gotten myself into another possible murder investigation.

"I don't know this mechanic Rusty personally," Jack said. "Probably because rescues always seem to happen after hours and we have our own crew to maintain the aircraft. But I know his reputation."

"Which is?"

"He's a hothead. People never know what will set him off."

"That's exactly what Britt said. She works at Spitfire."

"Okay, I'll make some calls, find out which plane he usually takes out and get a photo of it. If you saw it again, do you think you could identify it?"

"It was yellow. Not corn yellow or even lemon yellow. It was brighter, almost a glowing yellow. Like pee after you've taken too many B vitamins."

TMI?

Jack didn't seem to think so.

"Got it. Do you think you could stay under the radar for the next few days until I get some answers? Staying indoors would be ideal."

I gave him a wide-eyed stare that telegraphed, *um, no.*

"I figured. Please try to be safe, Halsey. I'd like you to be healthy and happy for our date on Saturday."

"Why? What do you have in mind?"

"You'll have to wait and see." He grinned.

"In other words, it's a surprise?"

He got a twinkle in his amber eyes.

I hate surprises.

CHAPTER 5

An impromptu Wine Club was called for the next day at Sally's to plan a course of action. When I walked onto her back patio with my bumps and bruises, it created quite a stir, so even before the first cork was pulled, I had told my dive bomber story.

Everyone was shocked.

I was excited to see two faces among the regulars, Jimmy and Britt. The patio around Sally's pool is an oasis of running fountains, fruit-bearing trees and African art. Everywhere you look, you find comfortable wicker chairs and sofas to lounge on. There's an ornate dream catcher that sways in the wind from the branch of an orchid tree. Bright, primary-colored umbrellas that adjust to the moving sun provide just the right amount of shade.

"I thought today I'd share some of my favorite Argentine, Don Miguel Gascón Malbec. Look for dark fruit flavors, chocolate and a hint of mocha. And a long, velvety finish," Sally announced, passing several bottles around to the group. "Let's celebrate none of us being in jail today!"

I saw the confused look on Britt's face and a few of the others and filled them in on our grisly discovery at the airport.

"Oh my lord, Jonas was such a sweet boy. I can't believe it. That explains why I didn't see him for lunch yesterday. He always comes in and orders a BLT on white. And to see me. He has—had—a bit of a crush on me. I discouraged it, but I must admit it was cute." Britt took a deep breath into her diaphragm and I noticed her eyes getting moist.

"I'm surprised it wasn't the talk of Spitfire Grill yesterday," Peggy said. "I know how fast news travels at that airport. Charlie's been inundated with calls and visitors from fellow pilots."

Peggy made a good point, and I looked to Britt for a response. It took her a few seconds.

"We were down a server yesterday and the hot weather brought out the noon crowd in droves. I barely had time to think, orders were piling up in the kitchen to go out. I never even came up for air until about three-thirty."

Yet she had time to notice Jonas wasn't there.

Britt drew a sympathetic nod from Aimee, who understood all too well the demands of being in the food service business.

"Poor thing, your feet must be killing you. Have some more wine. You may want to dangle your legs in the spa to loosen those muscles," Sally offered.

"I'm feeling better already, and I have two days off to rest up." Britt raised her glass in a toast.

"Jimmy, I'm so happy to see you home safe and sound," I said. "Can you fill us in on your field trip to police headquarters?"

"Not much to tell and it all happened so fast." Jimmy took a swig from the beer he'd been nursing. The deep circles under his eyes betrayed his nonchalant recounting of events. I could tell this had really rattled him.

"Give the girls the complete rundown, Jimmy. We've been known to solve a crime or two, and just because they released you doesn't mean you're off the hook." I noticed Sally sported the same dark circles.

"Right. It was a short drive to the station and the officers apologized for having to cuff me but did it all the same. Not the first time this has happened to me for doing nothing wrong, but you never get used to the humiliation and shame. And the fear that you're completely under someone else's control."

"I was put in a holding cell at the police station last year for a misunderstanding. I know that helpless feeling," I commiserated.

"They sat me in a room with one table, cameras on the ceiling and a wall with a mirror for unseen observers. Just like in the TV shows. But because they're all filmed here I guess that makes sense."

"There's that one they shoot in Hawaii, what's it called?" Aimee asked.

"Could it be *Hawaii Five-O*?" Peggy was also a fan of sarcasm.

"Please go on, Jimmy. I've done my share of crime reporting for the *Times* and I'll know if they violated any of your rights," Mary Ann assured him.

"Okay, but I don't think so. They told me I was free to go at any time, but they would appreciate it if I could answer some questions for them. What was I supposed to do? I'm from Chicago, so I knew to give short and very specific responses."

"What did they ask?" Sally had refreshed his beer.

"They had me run through the sequence of events again, starting with earlier in the afternoon, when I got the job and was given the grand tour. I told them about my brief meeting with Jonas along the way, really just an exchange of hellos and a couple of words about who we were."

"Who gave you the tour?" I asked.

"The curator of the museum, my boss. He's also the one who showed me the hangar where they do the restorations. He was hoping to introduce me to that fellow Rusty, but he was nowhere to be found."

"Did you meet any other people during this walk through?" Peggy was on the same wavelength.

"There were a couple of guys working on an engine, but we just waved to each other. I was never told their names. Same as I told the cops."

"Do you think it's possible one of the guys who was there during the day could have hung back to meet Jonas that night?" I knew this was a long shot.

"'Course it's possible, just like I told the cops. But I was told they give out keys to most of the people who work there, especially the engineers and mechanics, so there could have been lots of coming and going."

"You think Rusty has a key?"

"I know he does, Halsey."

Again, that proved nothing. "What else did the cops ask?"

"I finished with everything that happened when we returned that evening, and the guys stepped out of the room to confer for a minute."

"Did you tell them that we'd gone back specifically to talk to Jonas?"

Jimmy hung his head down.

"I'm sorry, Halsey. I didn't want to lie to the cops and have it come back to bite me."

"I completely understand, Jimmy. You did the right thing."

"Here, honey," Aimee said. "I've fixed you a plate. These are rain forest crackers, and that one has Humboldt Fog goat cheese on it. This is a Camembert with cranberry jelly, and these are fresh apricots."

Jimmy looked at her like she was speaking in tongues. Aimee can overwhelm you with kindness.

"When they returned," Jimmy continued, "I decided to talk first, say my piece. I told them if I'd had something to do with Jonas's death, why on earth would I return to the scene with witnesses to discover the body? It just made no sense."

"What did they say?" Britt jumped in.

"They agreed with me, for now. It seems pretty much everything is pending the results of the autopsy. They thanked me and drove me home."

"Did they mention any other suspects?" Britt pursued.

Britt's got more questions than an inquisitive two-year-old on a long car ride.

Jimmy shook his head. Britt had certainly taken an interest in this case, I thought. Maybe she was a mystery buff.

"I'll be very interested to hear those results. That poor guy died a brutal, savage death." Sally could say this as a former nurse with a clinical frame of mind. The rest of us shivered at the thought.

We all took a break to drink our wine.

Mary Ann broke the silence. "I do have a bit of good news."

We looked at her, anxious to hear it.

"Jeb's had a full battery of tests and he's a little anemic but otherwise fine. They are looking at his blood one more time—something about traces of a substance—but they've assured us that it's nothing serious. Also, they don't think his memory loss is any kind of precursor to dementia. It was more likely caused by dehydration and his low iron count. I'm feeding him steaks and chopped liver and he's as happy as a clam."

"That is great news, just don't let him around Charlie. He needs to lose a few pounds. I plan to take care of that when he's discharged from the hospital tomorrow. He'll stay with me until he feels strong enough to go home," Peggy said.

Sally looked at me, concerned. "You're being awfully quiet, Halsey. Very uncharacteristic of you. Are you feeling off your pegs?"

Off my what?

"I'm fine. But I think we need to take control of this investigation and our fates."

"Hear, hear," Jimmy concurred.

"I'm afraid I have to be going," Britt said. "My

shift starts in an hour and I need to clean up and sober up before then." She giggled.

"You'll be fine, honey. You're a great server." Aimee gave her a hug.

"Thank you so much. Sally, I love wine club!"

We watched her scamper off.

"Come back anytime," Sally shouted after her.

"I thought she said she had two days off?" Peggy whispered to me.

I looked at her. "Maybe starting tomorrow?"

We both shrugged, and I tucked that little conundrum into the back of my head.

"What's the plan, Halsey?" Mary Ann had pulled a small notebook out of her purse, ever the reporter.

"We have a number of nagging issues we need to get ahead of. Oddly, the least of my worries is you, Jimmy. Unless something really surprising comes from the autopsy, I'm guessing you'll soon be exonerated."

"Praise the Lord," he said.

"We've got the issue of Charlie's landing and what was on the runway that caused the crash. You believe him that he hit something, Peggy?"

"Damn right I do."

"Okay, it would seem the answers might rest with the elusive Rusty. Jack is going to follow up with his friends and contacts at the airport, but we should also look in to Rusty's personal life. Does he have a wife, girlfriend, any kids? Does he own a home? Have any debts? And what exactly makes Rusty such an angry guy? Sally, do you think you and Jimmy could do some digging into that? Do some online research, and Jimmy could subtly ask the people who work with him at the museum."

"You got it. I'm your girl."

"And I'm your guy!"

"Awesome. Peggy, we need to start working this whole prescription-drug angle. That's what concerns me the most. Maybe start with that airport Charlie flies out of in San Diego?"

"Montgomery, yes. Being so close to the border, it seems logical the drugs are brought into there for dispersion."

"I swear I didn't order those pills!"

"We know that, Sally, and we'll prove it. But there's also the much more serious matter of the heroin found in the fish. That smuggling crime comes packaged in a long stretch of prison time. We need to separate Sally, Charlie and Jimmy from that part of the bust as quickly and decidedly as possible. And soon."

I was pleased to see the mood get serious.

"I agree that is the big leagues, and so is the way Jonas was murdered," Peggy said.

"Do we know for sure it was murder?" Mary Ann asked.

"You were spared looking at the body; that was murder even if there were no external signs." My throat closed, remembering. "Peggy, I'm sure some of your old contacts from the job could help you with that."

"I know just who to call."

The other girls looked confused. Some were not around, and some may have forgotten, that when I first moved to Rose Avenue and ran into some trouble, it came out Peggy had done a brief stint with the CIA that involved a spy mission at the Santa Monica Airport in the early sixties. Yes, our sweet, dear Peggy. She called on some people from her past to help me prove my innocence, and for that I'll be eternally grateful.

But the fewer who knew about Peggy's ties the better, so I didn't elaborate.

"Aimee," I continued, "I am wondering about those fish. Were they just a charade to hide the drugs? Charlie said he's flown some before from time to time. It would be great to know if they're part of an actual legit order from a nearby restaurant, or even for personal consumption."

"Are you thinking this is some kind of recurring thing and the drug dealers have latched on to it?"

"I'm not sure, Aimee, but good question. We really need to find out what kind of fish these were. Augie will be of no help to me, but I've asked Marisol to work her magic."

"Her black magic, you mean. That woman is not of this planet." Peggy laughed.

"I did a story a few years back on the ease with which contraband can be transported within these small, municipal airports. There are no customs, no real checks and balances, unless a plane or entity is already under suspicion. I've got access to a wealth of data at the *Times*. I can start digging again."

"Mary Ann, that's fantastic," I said. "I feel so much better about everything than I did when we started Wine Club."

"We needed a plan and now we've got it," Aimee

declared, proud and teary. "The Rose Avenue Wine Club is on the case."

"Blow the expense, give the cat another gold-fish!" Sally said, opening a bottle of Bedrock "Ode to Lulu" California Rosé.

CHAPTER 6

To no surprise, when I returned home from Wine Club, Marisol was perched on my front stoop, her hawk eyes taking in all the Rose Avenue shenanigans.

"I'm pretty sure I have a restraining order against you being on my premises," I said as I plopped down next to her.

Today she was sporting denim gaucho pants, a blouse patterned with pink flamingoes and yellow garden clogs. She was just one zinc sunscreened nose away from being Señora Snowbird.

"I can leave if you don't want what I got for you."

She might as well have opened a box of See's Candies' Nuts & Chews and waved it under my nose.

"Okay, I'll bite. What have you purloined now?"

"I'm going."

"No, no, wait." I thought of English high tea

and changed my tone. "I am certain I would be unconditionally grateful for any information you are able to impart."

"It's not information, it's a thing."

"What thing?" I looked her over, but she appeared to be empty-handed, unless those pants had cavernous pockets.

"It's in my freezer."

I knew it was the wrong time of year for Christmas tamales, so she had my undivided attention.

"May I see it?"

"Thought you'd never ask." Marisol stood and headed up her driveway to the back gate.

I hate her.

"I'm keeping it in the freezer in my garage. It was too big to fit in the one in my house. I got a big ham in there for Easter, and that's also where I keep my nail polish."

As I followed her into the garage, I pictured ice trays nestling colored bottles arranged alphabetically from A to Z, starting with Absinthe Attitude and ending with Zinnia Zombie.

She tugged the door open and took out a package about the size of a Thanksgiving serving platter. It was covered in heavy foil.

"I was told to keep this frozen at all times," Marisol said while beginning the Russian doll unwrapping process.

Under the foil was a heavy freezer bag and then another layer of foil and so forth. She repeated this sequence five times before the item was revealed.

"Is that a fish? Did you get that from Augie?" I was ready to kiss her.

"Never mind how I got it and don't touch it. You can take a picture, though, for your research." She nodded with her chin to the cell phone I held in my hand.

I moved in for a closer look.

The fish was a silver color that turned to blues and turquoises when the scales caught the light. It wasn't more than a foot and a half long and had sharp dorsal fins that were high in front and tapered down as they went toward the tail. Like a Mohawk haircut. It wasn't the prettiest-looking fish I'd ever seen, but then again, if I'd been caught stuffed with heroin and then frozen, I might not have a good side either.

I opened my camera app and started snapping away. When I reached to turn the fish upright to get a shot of the full face, Marisol was quick to stop me.

"I said no touching!"

"I need to get this angle. It will help someone identify it!" I told her in no uncertain terms.

"I'll do it; you just take the picture."

Marisol retrieved some BBQ tongs from her grill and used them to set the fish on its belly. It wouldn't stay upright, so she had to keep her hold of it. Which meant that every shot I took also had her gold-tooth, smiling face in the background. I can't wait to find out what species the experts think Marisol is.

Note to self: Politely decline any invites from Marisol for a BBQ.

When I was sure I had enough photographic evidence, she reverse-engineered the unwrapping. You would think she'd found the missing link by the delicate way she handled the evidence. I hopped up

on an old dresser on the other side of the garag
and started an album for these photos. This piec
must have belonged to one of her girls because
was festooned with pink and purple My Little Pon
graphics and stickers. Bubbles surrounded the fig
ures depicted in them. Their scary large eyes an
enlarged pupils would have kept me up at nigh
all through grade school. Tell me that no drug
had been involved in the conception of this fran
chise and I'll sell you a case of inflatable ashtrays.

"You fall down drunk again?" Marisol asked, ey
ing my scraped knees and arms.

I repeated the story about being buzzed by
plane while up on the garden hill. I left out th
part about scaling a tree and my subsequent face
plant in the Santa Monica Mountains. Why worr
her?

"I can't help thinking someone involved wit
the airport did that to me on purpose. Maybe t
scare me off so I stop investigating the crash an
the murder. And the first person who comes t
mind is that guy Rusty. No one has a nice word t
say about him."

"That's the mechanic's name? Rusty? I know hi
mom. She works at the post office on Grandview
She always sneaks me to the head of the line whe
I have to send packages during the holidays."

"And how is that fair to the other people wh
are waiting patiently?"

Marisol just shrugged.

"Do you have to have a package to send to tal
to her?"

"I suppose I could stop by and bring her a co
fee. I probably owe her that."

"And then get the scoop on her son?"

"I could . . ."

I noticed she had her hand out, palm up.

"What?"

"Last I heard, coffee wasn't free."

"Jeez-us! Here." I gave her a five.

Her hand didn't budge.

"That has to be enough."

"You want her drinking alone?"

I took back the five and slapped down a twenty. It was all I had.

"I expect change, missy!"

"I'll also have travel expenses."

Shoot me now.

I was exhausted when I got home, but my mind was still racing. So many mysteries to unravel, and the clock was ticking. I had to believe whoever was trying to scare me off wouldn't just drop it. I was going to need to be much more clandestine with my investigation.

A forage through the fridge told me that an Italian antipasto salad was in order. Bardot got her usual two-course meal of kibble, then Greek yogurt with broccoli florets and carrots.

As I was slicing and dicing the salami, mozzarella, pepperoncini, and garbanzos, I thought about the inconsistencies in some of the things Britt had talked about today. Peggy had noticed them too. Something else struck me as odd as well.

"You had supper yet?" I asked Peggy when my cell phone connected.

Peggy added, "I was just staring into my freezer

hoping to find delicacies that simply required four minutes in the microwave. But all I see are Stouffer's French Bread Pizzas."

"Then come on over, I'm making dinner for the single ladies on Rose Avenue. Well, technically you're not single. You've got Charlie, but he's still in the hospital, so you're single tonight."

"Might I remind you that you've got Jack?"

"Not tonight, I'm making a big salad, Peggy, so come on by."

"On my way with a fresh, crusty bread and red vino."

Bardot was beside herself with delight when she saw who was coming to dinner. I sometimes think she and Peggy have their own way of communicating, a language made up of head cocks, gentle playing and transspecies pheromones.

"Bardot, have you been a model citizen today? Because if you have, I've got a carrot for you, freshly pulled from my garden."

Bardot looked at Peggy and lied through her teeth, adopting a submissive down state.

"And I brought a little something for you," Peggy added, handing me a bottle.

It was the perfect choice for this repast, a Ciacci Piccolomini d'Aragona Ateo red blend from Tuscany. This full-bodied, fruit-forward wine will stand up well to spicy sausage and tangy dressing. We sat at the table and went to town on our delicious dinner.

"What's eating you, Halsey? You don't seem your usual footloose and fancy-free self."

We'd finished our meal, chomped the last Italian-dressing-soaked crouton, and were finishing our Italian wine in the living room. Bardot was comfortably ensconced next to Peggy on the sofa, belly up, airing out her hoo-hah.

"I guess I'm off my pegs."

"What does that mean?"

"No idea. Sally said it to me."

"Ah, Sally-isms. I will never understand how someone with her intelligence comes up with such harebrained expressions."

"Hey, even the *Mona Lisa* has flaws. Look at her hands."

That got a laugh out of Peggy, and I relaxed a bit more.

"There are just so many unexplained actions and issues in this case, it seems impossible to tie them together."

"Maybe they don't all fit together," Peggy mused.

"Interesting. Let's break that down. The people smuggling the drugs certainly wouldn't have wanted Charlie's plane to crash, so they can't be the culprits who put something on the runway."

"Correct, unless it was put there accidentally. But we've still to determine if whatever it was had been put there by man or nature."

Peggy seemed to be sticking to her critter theory.

"I'm not sure how we get an answer to that." I felt my frustration rise again.

Peggy shifted her position on the sofa so Bardot could enjoy her fleeced bosom before she continued.

"Then we have the guy or gal who buzzed you with a plane. If you suspect Rusty, he'd have to have known you were aware of the drugs found. He was supposed to be home sick. Whereas everyone who was at Spitfire Grill that night knows you were one of people who discovered Jonas's body."

I took a sip of rich, red wine and considered that.

"Meaning the murder could be something entirely separate from the drugs. And until we have an estimate on time of death, we don't really know how many people could have had access to Jonas. Heck, that hangar is enormous. Someone visiting the museum during the day could have hidden in there until after they locked up for the night."

"Correcto-mundo."

Peggy was now in full CIA mode. As the story goes, her late husband, Vern, served in the Air Force and later worked at the Santa Monica airport, which was a crucial asset during wartime. The airport started allowing business jets to land and take off from there after WWII and the Korean War. The air force called in the CIA, who enlisted Peggy when they discovered a shipment of Russian weapons hidden aboard an aircraft they were servicing. Vern had recommended her. She claims it was only surveillance, and as a woman, she could get chummy with the pilots' wives for intel. They gave Peggy a special compact mirror and some other gadgets, but she says she never knew if she'd helped or not. At least, that's what she says. But Peggy admits she's only allowed to tell me a fraction of the story. No matter how much wine I ply her with, the rest of the story is buried deeper than Jimmy Hoffa. But she clearly learned to develop into an ace sleuth, and I trust her observations implicitly.

Peggy must have sensed I'd drifted away and did a pronounced clearing of her throat before continuing.

"Which means we need to find out what Jonas knew, did or said that would make someone want to kill him. Without that, the suspect list is practically endless," Peggy concluded.

"Britt seemed to have had some contact with him according to what she said at Wine Club. She implied he had a crush on her. Maybe it was reciprocal, and what we have here is a classic lovers' quarrel that turned deadly." I was reaching.

"That would be quite a leap from 'let's see other people.' I think I'll give her a call and ask her to help me prepare for the next Wine Club I'm hosting. I'll tell her this old lady could use some young inspiration and subtly extract information."

"I love it when you play the granny card, Peggy."

I went to the kitchen and got a glass of water, I was done drinking for tonight.

"Care for water?"

Peggy shook her head and savored her wine.

"So, are you going to say it, or am I?"

Peggy's question gave me a jolt.

"You mean, how much do we really know about Sally's cousin Jimmy?"

"Of course, I may be old but I'm not deaf, dumb and blind. You've had a wild hair up your caboose for most of the day. When you invited me to dinner that confirmed it."

"That's not why—"

Peggy dismissed my comment with a wave of her hand.

"Okay, I mean we have to look at this from every angle." I could feel my face heat up at saying that.

"True, but then we'd have to show some prior connection between Jonas and Jimmy. On the other hand, there's the matter of the envelope with the prescriptions that was addressed to Sally. Maybe Jimmy ordered them."

"See? Nothing adds up. Then there's Jeb. When he came into Spitfire he was so out of it, he could barely speak. His eyes were glazed over and distant. I'll admit he perked up after we got some fluids into him, but that was still a very strange incident."

"You think he's a boozer?"

"It didn't smell like it."

"And Mary Ann—she seems like an awfully smart cookie," Peggy continued. "She must have recognized how severe Jeb's condition was when Joe brought him home. Yet she seemed naïvely dismissive about the test results."

"You think she sugarcoated it to us?"

"It's possible. I'm curious about the substance she said they're going to test his blood for again."

It was time for me to fill Peggy in on Marisol's *sleuthing.*

"So, Jeb's intercepting packages from the mail carrier before Mary Ann can see them?"

"At least one, and it appears he was expecting a second the day of Charlie's crash."

I was feeling so much better having gotten this off my chest. Peggy has a way of getting people to talk.

"We're going to have to be careful how we handle this aspect. It could all be some kind of coincidence, and we wouldn't want to raise doubts where none exist."

"Agreed."

"Let's keep this between the three of us." Peggy got up to leave.

"The three of us?" I looked around, confused.

"You don't think she understood every word?"

Peggy pointed to Bardot. She was back to laying supine, her head and floppy ears hanging pink-side-out off the sofa's edge. A bit of her tongue poked out from behind her canines, which helped to facilitate her soft snores.

CHAPTER 7

The next day, I decided to embark on some online research for the contraband fish. I was in my office, sitting in front of my computer, something I needed to do more often for actual, wage-earning work. It was another glorious day in paradise, and I had all the windows and French doors open to let the breeze pass through, and I listened to a full-chorus concert from the sparrows hiding in the bougainvillea tree that hovers high over my pool. They perform every day and twice on Sundays. The only time I can remember them being silent for any period of time was when a brown-tailed hawk was circling the property. In typical eyes-like-a-hawk form, he spotted his quarry and swooped down to snatch it into his talons before disappearing into the top of a hundred-foot evergreen. The silence was palpable until I heard one sparrow say, "Shit, he got Jeremy." And that's why I never get any work done.

I first tried to identify the specimen in Marisol's freezer using my image search apps. Think Google, but instead of searching using words, you query with images. These are fun to use at a produce department when you spot an odd-looking fruit, but the database just isn't big enough yet to drill down to rare species of fish. Instead, I decided to look geographically starting with Southern California and then moving out. I set up a little query string program and then let it do its magic.

While that was running, I decided to do some small plane shopping. *Yellow* small plane shopping. Jack had wanted me to steer clear of the airport until he did some investigating on the plane that buzzed me, but that didn't need to stop me from doing a little digital digging. I started by reviewing photos taken at the Santa Monica airport and posted on their website in hopes of catching a glimpse of the offending aircraft. When that didn't pan out, I moved on to sites selling these planes.

I'd made notes on what I'd seen that day and reviewed them as I shopped. The wings were above the cockpit, and I learned that's what they call a parasol-winged aircraft. It had a single propeller on its nose. These types of planes arrived on the aviation scene around the start of the Depression and were popular until the mid-1930s. These planes were lighter in weight and cheaper to build. They were also very stable and gave the pilot better visibility from the fuselage. The plane I saw didn't look like an antique, which got me to thinking that perhaps this was a homebuilt job. That was the way to go if you didn't have a lot of money to spend. I was hot on the trail when Jack walked in the street-side door to my office and peered over my shoulder at the screen.

"Hey babe. I thought the plane research was my job," he said, kissing me. He looked handsome in his jeans and soft yellow silk shirt, which set his amber eyes into high beams. His lingering kiss made me forget all about planes.

It was then that I realized this was date night and my short shorts and Hitching Post tank just wouldn't do. I couldn't believe it was five o'clock. Time flies when you're plane shopping.

"I was just going to change. Pour yourself a glass of wine and I'll be right back."

"I'd rather watch you change," he teased.

"Then pour me a glass of wine anyway. I've got a yummy Australian blend open."

He met me in the bedroom with filled glasses and an eager spirit.

"Bardot is guarding the pool," he said.

I looked out the window and, sure enough, Bardot was lying at the far end of the yard, monitoring her watery playground.

Needless to say, we left a little later than originally intended, but neither of us seemed to mind.

"I've got to make one stop before we go to the restaurant, but it's on the way. It will only take a minute or so." I was the designated driver tonight.

We were heading toward Marina del Rey into the sunset—my favorite time of day.

"Why do I doubt that?"

"I just want to drop in on my Coast Guard friends to ask them if they recognize the fish from Charlie's plane. Trevor, the guy on duty tonight, is an avid angler and goes on trips down the California and Mexican coasts."

"I would love to do that, but not the sport fishing part. I'm all about catch only what you can eat. But the thought of a seafood crawl along the Baja Peninsula warms my cockles."

I laughed.

Again? This man is an animal!

The local Coast Guard was one of the first clients I won when I moved here. They needed an internal online system to share info and communicate during emergencies. I've since expanded the site's capabilities and made some great friends along the way. Plus, they rock at what they do.

We were headed to Marina del Rey, home to the yachts of the rich and famous as well as more modest houseboats and the practice waters for several collegiate and masters crew teams.

Along the main channel lie Fisherman's Village, a waterfront mall, a commercial boat anchorage and a tourist attraction with live-music concerts, restaurant and café dining, harbor and fishing cruises. And at the westernmost end is the Coast Guard station.

The sun had just started thinking about setting when we parked. The station was quiet when we walked in, but I figured this was just the calm before the storm. It was Saturday night, after all— boats and booze do not make for a happy couple.

"Hey Trevor. Fueling up for an evening of saving the overserved?"

He was chowing down on some delicious-looking shrimp tacos with rice and beans. I had to really focus on not rescuing that one shrimp that had fallen out and onto his plate.

"Hi Halsey, good to see you."

"We won't keep you from your supper; what I have to ask shouldn't take long. This is my boyfriend, Jack. You may remember him from the drug boat rescue and arrest a couple of years ago?"

"Sure do. How's it going, big fellow? Who are you in pursuit of now?"

"It's more Halsey than me, but then it always is."

The men shared a conspiratorial chuckle.

"The *who* this time is actually a fish. It was found on a plane flown by a friend of mine, and it was frozen and stuffed with heroin. I was hoping you could identify it for me."

I pulled up the photos on my cell phone.

"Yikes!" He gasped and pulled back from the photo. "Does that thing have two heads?"

"Ha! No, the one with the gold tooth belongs to my nosy neighbor, Marisol. Although I totally understand why you were taken aback."

He continued swiping through the photos and studied them carefully.

"I have some ideas. It's some kind of whitefish, but I've never seen this particular configuration in local waters. South America maybe?"

Not what I wanted to hear.

"Trevor's ruled out a lot of geography, Halsey. That should save us some time."

Jack was tugging on a spot on his beard, a sure sign he was uncomfortable and probably hungry. Those tacos must be getting to him too.

"My friend Shelly works at the Aquarium of the Pacific, I bet she could help you, or at least point you in the right direction. We dated for a short time, it didn't work out, but we've remained friends." Trevor opened the address book on his smartphone.

"That would be of enormous help, Trevor. I promise not to tell her that you just got engaged," I said.

"She knows; she'll be invited to the wedding. The fish and water world is a small one."

"That's what I'm always telling Halsey." Jack smirked, getting more and more antsy to leave.

"Okay, I just texted you Shelly's digits and I'll let her know you'll be calling. I hope it pans out. So, is someone going down for the drugs? I hope not your friend."

"Me too, Trevor. As usual, it's a lot more complicated than it first appeared, and several of my friends could be implicated. I've got to clear their names and get the cops looking in the right direction."

"If anyone can do it, you can, Halsey."

"Thanks so much, Trevor. I'm afraid your food's gone cold. Let me give you money for another order."

"No way. Hot or cold, it does the job. Good luck, Halsey; let's go fishing sometime, Jack."

"I'd love that."

"I love fishing too," I replied as Jack dragged me out of the station.

We drove back along Admiralty Way and turned in to the Marina del Rey Hotel. This establishment had been around for many years, but in the not too distant past it was a haven for rundown house-boat denizens known to drink too much, smoke too much and end up in dockside fights with their wives, girlfriends, mates and the errant pelican. The hotel had a happy hour every night and served hotel-pan, sterno-heated Swedish meatballs, egg rolls and pigs in a blanket. The frayed shag carpet was perpetually wet from the runoff from bathing suits and bare feet. But then an angel in the form of Pacifica Hotels took over and turned it into boutique accommodations with a restaurant called SALT that sits directly on the side of the Marina waterway.

The key is to go early, like we were tonight. Our table by the edge offered a front and center view of the sunset. Date night always kicked off with a cocktail, and a Moscow Mule was calling my name.

How to make vodka better? Add ginger.

Jack was feeling magnanimous and suggested we share the shellfish platter of Maine lobster, crab, oysters, prawns and Salt Creek mussels. Hot sauces and drawn butter completed the food porn picture.

Perfect.

After the initial gorge—I had to try one of everything—I could relax and talk.

"Okay, your plane research was confined to on-line, so I'll allow it into evidence," Jack began. "How about you tell me what you learned and then I'll share my info?"

Because technically what he said was true—I wasn't scheduled to meet a guy selling these plane kits until Monday—I proceeded.

"Can do," I mumbled between licking butter off

my fingers. Jack and I had that kind of relationship now. "The plane this guy was flying looked similar to the light planes from the thirties developed by a guy named Bernard Pietenpol. They had the same parasol-wing placement. You can buy reproductions today in the range of about one hundred and fifty thousand."

"That's a big nut," Jack said, going in for another oyster.

What? So I was counting; I'm an only child.

"Yes, that will buy a lot of oysters."

Jack took the hint and moved on to the shrimp.

"But if you're are an historic plane fanatic and must have a certain model, I found out you can buy the plans from Pietenpol Aircraft Company for about a hundred bucks and the aircraft-grade wood kits for the stabilizer, rudder, elevator, fuselage and wing for about three thousand. If you have resources for the hardware, engine and covering, I'm guessing you could be in the air for under twenty thousand."

"Wow, I'm impressed. You learn all this off the web?"

"I have a suspicion this internet thing might just take hold, Jack."

Ugh. Can the snark, Halsey.

Jack grimaced but recovered quickly.

"Here's what I've found, and it dovetails nicely with your theory. Rusty has worked at the airport since he was in his teens, so about fifteen years now. He had dreams of being a stunt pilot but always seemed to look for shortcuts through the system. I got this from an old-timer friend of mine over there."

"So he wasn't exactly rising up the aviation ladder?"

"Not so much. He also hung around with three guys who were a little older and would never pass up an opportunity to help themselves to plane parts or fuel when no one was looking. But apparently, one time someone *was* looking, and they were fired and banned from the airfield. Lucky for Rusty, he wasn't with them at the time, which doesn't mean he never participated in those thefts. It just means he wasn't caught."

"Interesting. Have you been able to find out if he owns a plane?"

"My guy suspects so, but Rusty got wise and stores it somewhere secret. I'll continue asking around and add your kit theory to the equation."

"We need to find that plane. At least that will solve one mystery. Our work is cut out for us," I said as we both eyed the last oyster. Jack made a grab for it, added some hot sauce and then fed it to me.

I have really got to start taking my love for this guy seriously.

"Hmmm," I said, savoring the transporting briny delicacy.

Jack grinned.

"Listen, Halsey, I've been thinking—"

"Now we need to track down where this heroin might have come from," I said, stepping on whatever he was about to say.

He looked at me with sad eyes for a moment.

"I'm meeting my friend Mark with the DEA for breakfast. I'll fill him in and see what information he can provide. They are probably already working the case."

I waved to our server and asked for a menu.

"You still hungry? I don't know where you put it!"

"I'd like to order a cheeseburger and fries to go, please."

He nodded, wrote it down and headed back to the kitchen.

"For Marisol?"

"For Trevor. Even if he ate his cold tacos, I bet he'll find a way to enjoy a warm serving of the major food groups, fat, potatoes and onions."

"You are very thoughtful, Halsey."

Jack was getting that faraway look again.

"What I said earlier, about taking a seafood crawl down the coast—let's really do that," Jack said. "We could maybe tie it into a celebration . . ."

I knew where this was going and tried to suppress the look of abject fear I felt forming on my face.

"Hmmm," I managed to utter.

"You know Malcolm and Penelope are getting hitched in September, and their winery is such a beautiful spot for a ceremony."

I instantly became afraid of where this was heading. That couple had met last year during the unfortunate circumstance of finding the old woman buried in my garden plot, and after a tumultuous beginning, they fell in love. Penelope moved to the winery, and with planning the wedding, we hadn't seen much of them lately.

"I'm not saying a double wedding, but maybe shortly after?" Jack was trying to evaluate whether he was delivering good or bad news.

"Is this a proposal, Jack?"

Lame. I need to work on my bob-and-weave skills.

He looked at the frozen smile I'd planted on my face and I saw his shoulders sag. Thankfully, our server appeared with the takeout and the check, so we both had a moment to recover.

"I think of it more as a proposal that we think about proposing." His hand had moved to his beard for a comforting tug.

I genuinely smiled this time. My gentle, amber-eyed giant was so giving in his earnest pursuit.

"I love that idea! But the deal is that either one of us can do the proposing when we feel the time is right."

"Wow. That makes me a happy man."

Mission accomplished, and I was feeling pretty good myself.

CHAPTER 8

The day started with lots of promise ahead, provided I got past the one little hurdle I needed to jump to set everything in motion.

"I'm going to need to borrow that fish. I promise to keep it frozen," I said to Marisol through the small openings in her black wrought-iron front security door.

"Can't."

I could barely make out her head in the shadow, and if it weren't for the glint off her gold tooth, I might have thought I was back in fourth grade confessing my sins to Father McCluhan.

Bless me, Father, for I have sinned. It has been one week since my last confession. I am deeply sorry I spit my lima beans into my milk at dinner so I didn't have to eat them.

"What do you mean, you can't? I've found someone who can identify the fish and she needs to see the real thing!"

"I promised, can't let it out of my sight."

I knew I was going to regret what I was about to say, but it would take a miracle to get that fish any other way.

"You can come with me. How exciting for you! I'm going to the Aquarium of the Pacific."

"I hate those places. Fish should be free to swim wherever the heck they want."

She wasn't going to make this easy, but I knew which Marisol buttons to push.

"You don't have to come in, I won't be long, and then I'll buy you a hot dog."

"You can't bribe me with food."

Since when?

She now had her hands on her hips and was staring me down. I weighed my options while I pictured Marisol at a craps table in Vegas with the high rollers. This one was playing like a pro. I knew my next offer needed to be big, and I needed to be prepared to walk away.

"So, the aquarium I need to go to is in Long Beach."

"So?"

It was my turn to string her along.

"So, there's something else that's pretty great in Long Beach."

"I've been to the *Queen Mary*. It was a long walk for a short drink of water, if you ask me."

Marisol was referring to the most famous steamship from the 1930s, which is docked in Long Beach, a revered historical landmark. You can tour this Art Deco masterpiece during the day or stay onboard in one of the cabins in the part of the ship that has been converted into a hotel. It's a favorite destination during Halloween due to the numerous eyewitness accounts of encounters with ghosts, particularly around the indoor swimming pool and boiler room. I could see why this wasn't Marisol's cup of tea; she prefers to be the haunter and likes her subjects to eat, breathe and make mistakes.

"I was not referring to the *Queen Mary*. This is much better."

I had her on the ropes.

"I don't care. You can't take the fish."

Ha! She folded too soon!

"Okay, then, never mind. Bardot is going to be awfully disappointed, though."

I stepped back from her door and headed home. I heard the clang of a heavy lock releasing and then the creak of her metal door.

"Wait. What about Bardie?"

"I didn't hear that."

"Bardot. What about Bardot?"

I stopped but kept my back to her just to make sure I'd set the hook.

"You made it clear you won't let me take the fish, Marisol."

"Maybe I can make an exception." She'd softened her voice to sweeten the statement.

"You sure?" I turned to her and she nodded.

"Okay, you get the fish. I've got a cooler all ready in the back of my car."

She let the door slam shut and I could hear her scampering across the kitchen to her backyard. All of a sudden, she stopped, and then I heard her scampering back to me. She got right up to the screen again.

"You still haven't told me what we're doing with Bardie, I mean Bardot," she demanded.

"After my meeting, we're going to Rosie's Dog Beach, of course! Don't forget your sunscreen."

"I don't burn," she hollered back at me in mid-scamper.

Come to think of it, I'd never seen her reflection in a mirror either.

That had been the clincher. Los Angeles city and county rules strictly prohibit dogs on the beach. People test the ordinance all the time, but if caught, the fines can be hefty. Rosie's is in the city of Long Beach, so it's zoned for off-leash four-legged frolicking in the sand and surf. I'd taken Marisol and Bardot there once before and it was dark before either of them agreed to get back in the car.

An hour later, we were finally cruising down the 405 freeway. Luckily, Shelly, the specialist I was meeting at the aquarium, had given me a wide window of time today. What was the holdup? Marisol decided to make lunch for a beach picnic, then couldn't find the high-powered binoculars she claimed were for whale watching but I know will be used for people spying. Finally, she needed to go through her batteries to find the ones that fit some other electronic device. She was keeping tight-lipped about its function for now.

"I went to the post office yesterday," Marisol announced from the shotgun seat.

"I'm proud of you. What do you want, a parade?"

"I brought coffees with me," she continued, ignoring my snark and grinning. This beach trip had put her in a solidly good mood.

"You talked to Rusty's mom! So, what did you find out?"

"Her boy's a no-good mess, but she claims he has a good heart."

"A mess in what way?"

"Owes a bunch of money. When he started out at the airport, he had plans to become a famous pilot. She says that was all he talked about, bragged all the time to his girlfriend that they'd get married and travel all over the world."

"I have a feeling I know where this story is going."

We'd just passed the airport traffic and were now cruising at a comfortable speed for Los Angeles. It was a weekday and we were dealing with a rare heat wave that was keeping people indoors even at the beaches.

"She says when things weren't moving as quickly as he'd liked, Rusty started taking matters into his own hands. Like cheating on some written pilot's tests and getting in with a bad crowd of losers at the airport. She told me that he'd also never realized how expensive it was to fly. Rusty was always hitting her up for money. When the well ran dry, she suspects he turned to illegal ways to get the cash."

"Like dealing drugs?"

"She didn't say exactly, but she gave me the universal sign."

"Which is what?" I was afraid to look.

"I don't remember exactly, but you know it. Something like this."

Marisol pantomimed making a fist with her thumb sticking out and bringing it to her lips as if she were drinking, followed by pinching her thumb and index finger together in front of her face like she was smoking, and for her denouement she crossed her arms dramatically.

I had no comment, but Bardot thought it was a great game and started licking Marisol all over. When that wasn't enough, she tried to climb into the front seat with us.

"Don't make me pull this car over," I yelled.

"Sorry, Bardie, your mom's cranky when she doesn't have her wine."

I swear, I saw Bardot laughing in my rearview mirror.

My cell phone rang, and I turned on the Bluetooth speaker on my steering wheel.

"Hi honey."

"Hi babe, you driving?"

"I'm headed to the Aquarium of the Pacific, I have Bardot and Marisol with me."

"Two of my favorite girls."

"Who's that?" Marisol asked.

"It's Jack. You think I call anyone else honey?"

"Probably when you drink."

"Listen, I've only got a minute," Jack continued, "but I saw Mark this morning and, as I suspected, the DEA is all over the heroin found in the fish on Charlie's plane. He says it's part of a really bad batch that's been circulating for the last few months and putting a shocking number of naïve millennials in the hospital for overdosing. He says it's cut with fentanyl, making it a dangerously strong narcotic. Fifty times more potent than morphine."

"Yikes, those poor kids." And parents, I thought.

"The DEA is working on sourcing the origin of the fish, but these things, especially operations outside the U.S., can get bogged down in bureaucracy. I would say you all are on a very important mission and time is of the essence to clear your friends. Gotta go, love you."

Jack clicked off.

"I knew he loved me." Marisol beamed.

"*What?*"

"I suppose I could leave the car running so you two get the cool air," I said to Marisol after we'd parked at the aquarium. I'd opened my window to test the temperature and felt like I'd stuck my head in the oven to check on the Thanksgiving turkey. I'd quickly closed it back up.

"You're trying to kill us, aren't you?" Marisol said this more like a statement than a question.

"When we left, I figured that you and Bardot would maybe walk around outside and watch the boats and birds dockside. I had no idea this heat wave was going to continue and it would feel like a sweat lodge."

I had to think this through. As Jack had said, I was on an important mission. Behind me, Bardot smelled sea critters and wondered what was taking us so long. I dialed a number on my phone, which was still hooked up to the car's Bluetooth.

"Hi, this is Shelly," came the response. We could hear running water and ambient noises in the background.

"Hi Shelly, it's Halsey."

"Great, you're here, I'll meet you at the information desk on the ground floor."

"Um, there's one thing—" I started to say.

"Oh?"

"I have my dog with me, as well as my neighbor. They were going to wait outside while we met, but we hadn't planned on it being this hot a day."

"Hmmm. The aquarium has strict rules about this. Only service dogs are allowed inside. Does your dog qualify?"

I paused for a second while my good Halsey and bad Halsey battled it out.

"Why yes, she does," I finally declared.

"You're going straight to hell," Marisol said.

When the three of us entered the aquarium, we stopped to take in the environment. Just like I felt when I pulled onto my Mar Vista home for the first time, I felt like I was in Oz and had Toto in tow, along with the Wicked Witch of Rose Avenue. All around us were people in sea-blue polo shirts smiling and asking if they could help us. In front of us, taking up most of the back wall, was the aquarium's version of the Wizard's palace. A floor-to-ceiling, glass-exposed tank called the Blue Cavern was teeming with all shapes and sizes of sea life and flora. You didn't know where to look first. A diver had lowered himself down from the top and was hand-feeding the fish, while a dry-land expert

provided commentary to the large group of uniformed third graders here on a school trip. They
formed a rapt semicircle in front of the tank.

A wave from a staff member caught my eye, and
I figured this must be Shelly, signaling us to come
over. For once, Bardot was well behaved, probably
overwhelmed by sensory overload and feeling very
much like a dog out of her pool. Plus, we'd had a
little talk before we entered the building, and I'd
told Bardot and Marisol exactly how I expected
them to act, because we were guests. At least one
of them seemed to be listening.

"You must be Shelly," I said, extending my hand.
"This is my neighbor, Marisol, and my service dog,
Bardot."

"Hah!" Marisol didn't even try to control herself.

"Never mind her," I whispered to Shelly. "Her
age is advancing but her mind is regressing. I just
thought a day out would do her some good."

Shelly nodded and gave my back a soft rub. She
approved of my altruism.

"This way, ladies. We're going to go through the
staff door and take the elevator to the second floor."

We followed obediently, knowing she was the
alpha dog in this scenario. Shelly did have a com-
manding presence, and not just because she was
tall. Her long, California-blond hair came down almost to her waist and was held neatly in place with
a low ponytail. I guessed her to be in her late twen-
ties or early thirties and suspected her naturally
blushed cheeks and dark lashes would bless her
from having to wear makeup her entire life. Her
body was trim but athletic, and knowing my Coast

Guard friend Trevor, she could probably match him toe-to-toe paddleboarding, surfing or waterskiing. She had a warm, assuring smile that made me feel safe.

"We're going to go to the area above the Blue Cavern," she explained as we boarded a very large elevator that could transport a shark. And from the odor inside, I imagined this happened often. "I'm running backup for the feeding show you saw going on for the kids, so I have to be on stand-by in case they need anything. I'll examine the fish there," she said, nodding to the Playmate cooler I was carrying.

"Great. As I said on the phone, I don't want to take up too much of your time. I'm so grateful for any help we can get."

"No worries, I'm fine," Shelly said as we disembarked. "Your dog is so good, I'm impressed."

"Ha!"

This time Shelly responded by throwing an arm over Marisol's shoulders and gently leading her into the space. When we entered, we could hear the commentator's voice being piped in. Shelly worked a button and turned the sound down a bit.

"We'll stay up around the perimeter of the tank and behind the railing," Shelly explained.

We followed her to a built-in shelf along a back wall. It had a grate over the top of what I could now see was a basin for water and any fishy bits to drain. In the center of the room, water circulated in and out of the top of the Blue Cavern. We watched with fascination as curious fish swam up to the surface, looking for food, and then dove back down when they didn't find any. Bardot's eyes were as wide as saucers.

"So, we have a mystery to solve? I understand. One of my favorite things to do. I remember back when we ran into a puzzle ourselves. We started noticing that some fish would go missing from one of our galleries. Gone without a trace, so we ruled out any predators in the same tank. We wondered if someone was stealing them to sell on the black market, so we set up a camera to film the display throughout the night. The next morning, when we reviewed the footage, we found the culprit."

"Was it aliens?" Marisol asked. The story was about spying, her favorite subject.

"Close. It was an octopus from the neighboring tank. It would scale over the rim when it got dark and help itself to a seafood buffet. That's why we now keep lids on all the octopus aquariums. Turns out, a lot of places were experiencing the same thing."

I watched Marisol mull this over and could just see her at the computer tonight, searching for mail-order six-armed cephalopods.

"Let's take a look at the specimen, shall we?"

Shelly brought me back to the business at hand, and I opened the cooler. Marisol was quick to reach in and hand Shelly the fish, preserving the chain of custody in her mind, I assumed.

Shelly turned on a flexible overhead light and bent it down close to the fish for examination. She donned some latex gloves and rinsed the fish in warm water to soften it a bit. Shelly used a pair of long-nosed tweezers to lift the gills and open the mouth. Each time she looked in a new place, Marisol gave out an *uh-huh* like this was exactly what she had expected. I gave her the evil eye behind Shelly's back.

"It's a tilapia," she finally said, removing her gloves. "I'm going to scan our database to see if I can narrow it down more. Based on the strength of its fins, this looks to be a warmer-water fish. Meaning it isn't from the coast of California or even Mexico but someplace closer to the equator. Maybe Nicaragua? I'm seeing species that are close but none that are spot-on," she said, scrolling through her computer pages. "That makes me wonder if this could be a freshwater specimen, and the only way to confirm that is through DNA testing."

"Is that a big deal to conduct?" I asked, thinking back to all the tedious testimony I watched in the O. J. Simpson trial.

"No, but it will take about a week for the results to come back. I'd like to hang on to the fish until we're done."

I saw Marisol's mouth open and quickly shut it and turned her to face the pool.

"Look at all those pretty fishies, Marisol. Don't you just love them?"

"With tartar sauce I do."

"Shelly? Come in," squawked her radio.

"I'm here, Angelina. What's up?"

"The giant sea bass are a bit lethargic today and the kids are getting restless. Do you think you could send down some delectable crustaceans?"

"On their way."

Shelly walked over to a freezer and pulled out a

bag of shrimp. "This will just take a minute," she said to us.

We watched her walk down some concrete steps that were partially submerged in the water. She started strategically tossing in shrimp around the edges where she must have known the bass were hiding.

"I'm taking my fish home with me." Sunny, happy Marisol was gone.

"No, you're not. And now it's *your* fish?"

"Yes, I am. I promised Augie."

"Since when do you keep any of your promises?" I realized I was raising my voice.

"Since I'm in charge of the fish."

"You know the cops removed the heroin, right?"

"Still takin' it."

Splash.

I'd been so engrossed in arguing with Marisol that I hadn't noticed I'd let Bardot's leash slip out of my hand. And true to form, she dove into the tank to retrieve a shrimp Shelly had tossed in.

Over the loudspeaker, I could hear the commentator say, "We seem to have a new species of dogfish," over the squeals and cheers from the kids.

"Shelly, what is going on?" came an angry voice on her radio.

Bardot emerged with shrimp in muzzle and climbed a couple of steps before shaking water all over Shelly.

"She's no service dog, is she?" Shelly looked up at me, furious.

"She saved that shrimp, didn't she?" Suddenly, Marisol decided to get involved.

"I'm so sorry. This is my fault. Just let me know

who I should explain this to. I don't want you to get in any trouble."

"I think it's best if you get your dog out of here as quickly as possible, Halsey. I'll call you when I have the test results."

"Of course. Come on, Marisol."

"I want my fish."

"You'll be sleeping with the fishes if you don't follow me right now," I said, dragging her to the elevator.

CHAPTER 9

The next morning, Jack and I walked over to the Santa Monica airport in the hopes of springing a surprise visit on Rusty. I'd called Jack when we got home last night to let him know Bardot needed a training refresher course. I thought he'd never stop laughing when I described Bardot the diving dog's escapades.

We checked in with Officer Leo, supervisor at the police substation, and he offered to come along to ensure there wasn't any trouble.

"Thanks, Leo, but I'm afraid seeing you would just make Rusty very quiet and uncooperative. Have you had any issues with him in the past?" This man had a proud barrel chest and a generous ability to listen.

"Rusty has always stood on the periphery of any real infractions, but I suspect he's pulling the strings in the background. He wasn't always like this. As a kid, he was gung ho about aviation and becoming a pilot. But some bad luck gave him an attitude that was probably always beneath the surface. Such a shame."

"I agree," said Jack. "Where would we find Rusty at this time of day?"

Leo walked out a side door to the observation deck overlooking the runways.

"See that hangar across the way? We keep supplies and have a workshop housed in there. Rusty treats it like his own private office. You'll need to look in the back corners, but that's where he'll be. I'll drive you around the field; you can't just go walking across two runways."

Off we went in an open-air golf cart.

We thanked Leo for the lift and entered the space. I don't know why these hangars feel so creepy to me, but this one was no exception. The outside sunlight only stretched about ten feet into the cavern, and after that it was black as pitch. It was hard to gauge how deep the structure was.

"Hey, Rusty?" Jack's voice echoed and was followed by silence.

I took out my cell and turned on the flashlight app. It got us about another four feet of light.

"Rusty?" I tried, thinking of the bees/honey approach.

We heard the unmistakable sound of a gun being cocked and froze.

"We just want to talk, buddy," Jack said, slowly moving in front of me to form a human shield.

I really should marry this guy.

We heard a deep hum of power as big ceiling lamps illuminated at the back of the hangar.

"Over here," said a voice.

Jack gave me a signal to stay behind him and follow. Just like Leo had suggested, we found him in the far-right corner at a workbench. We approached with our hands up.

"Whoa, what's that for?" he asked, seeing our surrender posture.

"You have a gun?" Jack asked slowly, lowering his arms. "We heard one cock."

"No. Why would I have a gun? And who's *we?*"

"That would be me," I said, appearing from behind Jack's massive torso.

His look of surprise seemed genuine.

"I'm Halsey and this big fellow is Jack. We're trying to help our friend, Jimmy. He's the guy who discovered poor Jonas's body."

Rusty pushed back his straight, sandy-blond hair from his eyes but otherwise showed no emotion. He was tan, on the thin side and looked much more like a middle-aged surfer than a pilot. He stood frozen in place, unsure of his next move or ours.

"We were hoping you could tell us a little about Jonas." Jack settled down on a bench along the back wall, hoping to show we only came here to talk.

I watched as Rusty's shoulders relaxed.

"I don't know what happened to the kid. Pretty scary stuff," Rusty said, opening a folding chair for me.

I'd have to remember to tell Marisol to pass along to his mom that he hadn't forgotten his manners.

"Was Jonas involved in any substance abuse you know of, Rusty?" Jack asked.

"Doubtful, but you never know."

This guy is just gushing with information.

"What was Jonas like? Was he from here originally? Did he want to fly? Is that why he signed on to work for you?" I hoped this would focus his responses.

"He didn't just work for me, he worked for the airport. Management hired him. Not sure where he's from originally, but there's one thing I do know."

"What's that?" This was like pulling teeth.

"That kid loved flying. He couldn't wait to get his license. But his impatience was going to bite him in the butt. You can't rush the steps."

I looked at Jack. We both knew that Rusty was speaking from experience.

"On the day of Charlie's crash, who was working here to receive incoming flights?" Jack picked up the questioning.

"I was supposed to be. I came in to process the cargo that had been delivered the night before. But something I ate had just chopped me off at the knees. I was hurling every few minutes and couldn't even keep water down. I noticed Jonas poking around back here and decided to let him take over. There were only a few planes scheduled for that day. I figured it was okay."

"Do you regret that decision now, given the accident on the runway?"

"Hell no!" Rusty glared at Jack. "That tarmac was clean when I left. It wasn't possible for anything to cause an accident. It was pilot error, plain and simple. Those guys just never want to admit they make mistakes, especially the old dogs."

He picked up a socket wrench off the worktable and threw it across the room.

"I got stuff to do. Is that it?"

Jack nodded, taking my elbow to steer me out of harm's or temper's way.

"Just one more question," I said, and both men groaned.

"Who owns that gorgeous yellow Pietenpol? I just love it!"

He paused for a moment and stared at me.

"No clue," he said and walked away.

On the way home, we stopped at Spitfire for a quick lunch. We both ordered the special, blackened fish tacos.

"It seemed pretty clear to me that Rusty was holding a lot back from us, which makes me even more suspicious." I was trying to nibble daintily but failing miserably.

"Yes, but the question is why? He seemed pretty twitchy, almost a little spooked. And not by us. When we settled down to talk to him, he seemed to relax a bit." For each bite of taco, Jack used one paper napkin to mop his beard. I realized I'd never seen him eat corn—

"You think someone else was back there?" I asked.

"Or had just paid him a visit. Once he flipped the lights on, it would have been hard to remain out of sight."

"But not impossible. You still sure that was a gun we heard being cocked, Jack?"

"One hundred percent." He took his last bite

and thought for a minute. "But maybe the gun wasn't for us. He could have been pointing it at the person who had paid him a visit, and the sound we heard may have been the gun being de-cocked."

He was right, of course, making this an even bigger challenge to decipher.

"I think we need to divide and conquer. Rusty swears there was nothing left on the runway when Charlie landed, and he has no reason to lie. He said he'd gone home sick and left Jonas in charge. If anything *was* there, he could blame Jonas."

"Correct, so why'd Charlie make such a big deal out of it? Pride, maybe? It's sad to think his flying skills are waning."

I nodded. It was starting to seem that the runway crash was a catalyst to setting everything that happened afterward in motion. If I could figure out what caused it, I'd have a lot more pieces to the puzzle.

"Did you catch Rusty saying he'd come in early to unload cargo from the night before? I wonder what that was. Do you think you could find out who flew in at that time and from where, Jack?"

"Consider it done. We'll solve this, Halsey."

"We'd better do it soon. So far, we've come up with nothing to prove Sally and Jimmy are innocent."

"We haven't found anything to prove they're guilty either."

"Dear Jack, the glass half-full attitude only works at Wine Club."

He grinned and gave me a kiss.

"Babe, I've got to boogie. I'm running a clinic in less than an hour."

"Go. I've got this."

I got another kiss and watched him leave. On the way out, he ran into Britt, and they chatted for a minute. I signaled my server for the bill.

"Hi! I just met your gorgeous boyfriend."

"I saw. How are you doing, Britt?"

"I'm good. How are Sally and Jimmy? Did everything get cleared up?"

"Not yet. I'm afraid Jimmy's still on the hook with the police. But Charlie's on the mend, and he went back home to San Diego today. Peggy's throwing a Wine Club this afternoon to celebrate having the house back to herself. You should come."

"Charlie's from San Diego . . . I can't do Wine Club today."

That was awfully emphatic.

"Britt, are you going to work today?" asked the manager on duty. "You're already forty minutes late and we're about to get hit with the lunch crowd."

"Oops, got to go. Nice seeing you, Halsey."

Britt doesn't seem like the type to be late . . . and didn't she say she had these two days off?

The afternoon was nigh, and just like feeding time at the zoo, a new energy was radiating over Rose Avenue. Five women heard the call and stopped whatever they were doing. It was time for Wine Club.

"He swears on a stack of Bibles he hit something on that runway," Peggy announced while giving me a generous pour of Norton Reserva Chardonnay from Argentina.

The heat wave was gone, so we gathered in her living room, where she had the plantation shutters perfectly arranged so we could see everything happening on Rose Avenue, but no one could see in.

Peggy's pristinely clean house shows off her four kids and twelve grandkids, as seen in the framed collage of photos that hang on her wall. She still lives in the house she got married in on Rose Avenue.

As the story goes, the night Peggy became a widow, she and her husband, Vern, were throwing a dinner party. Thankfully, he slumped over peacefully at the table and went to heaven. Everyone stayed while the coroner came and, after, slowly started to leave. Reportedly, Peggy asked where everyone was going. Vern would never want to break up a party! They drank until dawn, telling story after story about him. A flag flies at Peggy's house every day and comes inside at dusk, homage to Vern's Air Force career. The days were getting longer, so the Stars and Stripes were still in the honor position on the front of Peggy's house. I smiled at the thought of that devotion, and then glanced at Sally, who sat quiet and withdrawn. It reminded me how urgent our mission had become.

"Let's assume Charlie did hit something, and we'll keep working on what and how it disappeared later. Peggy, did Charlie tell you anything about the ice cooler, where he picked it up, what he was told was inside?" I asked.

"Yes," she said, blowing on a pig in a blanket before popping it in her mouth.

She very quickly made a wide O with her mouth and fanned the opening with her hand. Aimee ran into the kitchen for a glass of water. The rest of us were poised to dial 9-1-1 or hand her a napkin to spit the little heat bomb into. She finally chewed and swallowed.

"Here, honey," Aimee said, handing her a tall glass of H_2O.

"What am I going to do with that?' Peggy stared at her.

"Cool down and soothe your mouth."

"I've got wine for that. Charlie said he'd heard about the seafood delivery just before takeoff. He told me a waiter from the Mexican restaurant on the airfield at Montgomery-Gibbs brought it to the plane. He didn't get the guy's name, but I'll keep bugging Charlie until he does. Some of us may need to make a trip down there."

"I think you're right about that, Peggy. Jack and I paid Rusty a visit this morning. He didn't tell us much, but he did mention that the morning of the crash he came in early to deal with some cargo that had arrived overnight. Maybe the two shipments are connected somehow. Jack is working on tracing the cargo and I'm going to solve the runway issue no matter what."

Thinking back to the hangar gave me a chill, and I shook visibly.

"Something else spook you about that meeting, Halsey?" Peggy had her spy hat on.

"I'm trying to convince myself I didn't hear what I heard."

"What's that?" Mary Ann looked at me, concerned.

"When we entered the hanger, it was pitch black inside. Jack called out Rusty's name, and from the deep back end we heard a gun cocking."

"Oh dear Lord." Aimee slumped down in her chair. "I hope you ran right back out."

"Actually, Jack moved in front of me in case any bullets went flying, and we explained our visit. Rusty relaxed enough to turn on the lights. He said he didn't have a gun. Jack suggested we could have heard a gun being decocked and maybe it was meant for someone else."

"Did you manage to get a good look around back there? See anything we can pin on the egg-suckin' dawg?"

I shook my head at Sally.

"Then the hangar's also probably worth us paying a visit to in the near future," Peggy said, impaling a wine cork.

Aimee stood.

"I can report on the seafood served at Spitfire Grill." Aimee picked up the ball. "I don't know if this is good news or bad, but they've been buying from the same warehouse in Long Beach for years. Even for special dinners, that's where the fish is sourced. Britt was amazing in how fast she got the information for me. She's such a honey."

Peggy and I exchanged looks as she passed around a tray of cream-cheese-stuffed Bugles. Peggy really kicked it old school when it came to appetizers. I wondered how much we could trust Britt's intel, but it was easy enough to check. She'd be risking a lot if she was lying.

"I'm so happy I can finally contribute," Mary Ann piped in. "As I said before, these small municipal airports aren't subject to the same security measures that the larger ones are. The key is to follow the noise restrictions, and if you're flying a plane like Charlie's, as long as you fly VFR, the FAA doesn't require you to file a flight plan."

"VFR?" I asked.

"Valid flying registration?" Sally suggested.

"Very fine ride?" Aimee proffered.

"Visual flight rules. It means the pilot can see out of the plane to navigate, avoid hitting other planes and maintain a desired altitude," Mary Ann clarified. "Hal, who covers this type of thing at the *Times*, tells me there are no customs checks, and unless the authorities have prior knowledge of suspicious cargo arriving, people land their planes and take whatever they have onboard on and off as they please."

"Wow, that leaves room for a lot of slippery business." Sally shook her head. "Maybe I will start getting my prescriptions from Mexico, at least some of them."

Mary Ann's cheery expression fell at the thought of that, and she sighed.

"I may have some information on the medicine part of Charlie's delivery, but I don't want to say any more about it right now until I run down some leads."

We all stopped eating and drinking when Mary Ann dropped that intriguing nugget.

"Come on, tell us what you're thinking," Peggy teased her.

"No," I said, "I think it's best we keep to what we

know. Mary Ann will tell us when she's ready with solid information."

I then took them through my trip to the aquarium, which lifted their moods immensely, less for any discoveries I'd made but more for Bardot's comic relief. I certainly have a story to pull out if I'm ever stuck in an elevator.

"Shelly is going to call me when she gets the DNA results back. When we met, she suggested the fish might come from fresh water in places like Nicaragua, so I'm going to start researching that angle on the web."

"That at least sounds like some progress is being made, although I still feel that Jimmy and I could be arrested at any moment. It's the curse; it's back, I just know it."

"You keep mentioning that, Sally. Care to fill us in?"

"Peggy lived through it. She remembers as well."

Peggy gave a solemn nod. "It was one week of hell."

"Oh my God, you're scaring me." Aimee was both wide-eyed and teary, not an easy feat.

As a precaution, we filled one another's wine-glasses before circling closer around Sally and Peggy.

"First off, it rained for five days straight, which in and of itself wasn't a bad thing. We always need the water," Sally began.

"The problem was the lightning. It struck a palm tree and knocked out the power for the entire block. Now that I think about it, the tree was on your property, Halsey."

I didn't know why, but Peggy's realization made me uneasy.

"That's right," Sally picked up. "The Hollenbacks were living there back then. They fought continuously, and we thought God was trying to teach them a lesson. The garage burned, along with their cars, they moved soon after and the new owner built what is now your office."

It dawned on me that the spot in my backyard where I could never get anything to grow must be where the palm once stood.

"My neighbor Danny was recovering from a broken kneecap he'd suffered in a surfing accident. He just had to go out in those prestorm big waves. He was hooked up to a machine for electronic bone stimulation, and when they couldn't restore power right away, I had to take him back to the hospital. It was on the way home that I had my car accident."

"Oh my, Peggy. What happened?" Aimee reached for her hand and proceeded to check her body for telltale scars.

"A damn cat, that's what happened."

"It was more than a cat; there was a chain of events sort of like a Rube Goldberg device, where one small thing triggered another and another, and half an hour later, your toast was buttered. And cold." Sally was clearly on the shortest distance between two points side.

"Right. I was driving along the west perimeter of the Santa Monica airport and I guess water had been building up at that end of the runway. Suddenly, it overflowed, causing a mudslide on the hill and into the road. I swerved to avoid it, but the car behind me wasn't so lucky. It hydroplaned and ran into a street sign, knocking it over. I tapped my brakes so I could stop my car and go for help. That spun me around. I was then facing oncoming traffic." Peggy drained her wineglass, parched from her tale.

"And that was when the cat—"

"Not quite yet, Halsey," Sally continued. "I was heading back from Bob's Market. I'd picked up the prime rib roast I'd ordered for Joe's birthday."

"They have the best meat department," Aimee gushed nodding her head as she thought about it.

"By that point, the road had turned into a shallow river, with just enough water to make it impossible to control your car. I was on a collision course with Peggy."

"I figured I had one chance and took a sharp right into the alley, narrowly avoiding hitting Peggy. My car stopped on the incline and I got out to rescue Peggy."

"At that point my car had stalled," Peggy continued the story. "When Sally opened my side door to pull me out, a cat jumped in to get out of the rain and I jumped out of my seat in fear. I recoiled, and I must have knocked the car into gear. The street sign that had been knocked into the cat's yard must have spooked him. Sally quickly lunged in and across my lap, her feet hanging out the door as we rolled backward down the hill all the way onto the golf course."

"We both spent the next three hours in St. John's ER. Thankfully, I knew some of the girls on duty that day, and we were put in a room right away."

"Wow. That's a lot for one week. I can see why you call it a curse, Sally."

"That wasn't the end of it." Mary Ann now had the floor and our undivided attention.

"I was just a teenager and we lived on the western end of Rose Avenue. There was an eighty-year-old lady who lived alone across and a few houses down the street. As I was waiting for the school bus one morning, I saw the nurse who looked in on her each week go into the house. About a minute later, I heard a horrible scream. I'll never forget it."

"That was that same week. I'll be darned," Peggy reflected. "The poor dear had been knocked out. It was a botched home robbery, as I recall. They never did find out who did it."

"Thankfully, she recovered," Mary Ann continued. "But she could never stand to spend another night in that house. She moved back East to live with a relative. They did catch the guys, thirty-five years later! I know because I worked on the cold case at the *Times*. The cops managed to match DNA from a recent crime to that found in the old lady's house. It was two kids who were sixteen and seventeen at the time, and they're finally behind bars."

"Bravo, Mary Ann." I had to marvel at my talented group of friends. Her mention of DNA testing made me wonder if any was done on the envelope addressed to Sally with the prescription drugs.

"I'll never forget the sign outside the cold case office downtown. It said, *A city that forgets its murder victims is a city lost. This is where we don't forget.*"

"That was beautiful, Mary Ann. I sure hope if we have been going through a curse we've kicked its butt to the door." Aimee kicked the air, just in case.

Not yet, sweet Aimee.

Sally's cell phone rang.

"It's Augie. I'll put him on speaker. This is Sally, and I've got the group with me as well. What's the news?"

We all held hands.

"We finally have a cause of death for Jonas, ladies. Without any outward physical signs, we had to run a series of toxicology panels. He was poisoned by a lethal injection of a high amount of scopolamine."

"What's scopolamine?" I asked, and everyone nodded with the same question.

"I know it as hyoscine. It helps with postoperative nausea and can decrease saliva if administered prior to surgery," Sally the nurse told us.

Peggy and I both covered her mouth to prevent her from saying anything more. *No need to fuel Augie's fire.*

"I figured you would have heard of it, Sally. In the Colombian drug world, it's also called 'the Devil's Breath' because it causes the user to be devoid of free will, hallucinate and be highly susceptible to the power of suggestion. People empty bank accounts, commit crimes, they've even been known to sell an organ."

"Jeez," Peggy said, and then remembered to keep quiet.

"The same drug that's used in hospitals does these

horrible things to people?" Aimee asked, and I knew what she and Tom would be discussing at dinner tonight.

"I was told that the difference is how it's extracted and processed. It comes from the borrachero tree, which grows wild in that part of South America. The DEA recently busted the owners of a nightclub who were using the drug as an added bonus for their male patrons to seduce women."

"What does all this have to do with us, Augie?"

"Nothing, which is why I called Sally, not the rest of you."

"I don't like the sound of this. Give it to us straight," Peggy demanded.

"Okay, one of the mechanics at the airport came forward and told us that he'd heard Jimmy and Jonas having a heated discussion the afternoon before he was found dead. Another guy corroborated the story. They couldn't clearly make out what the guys were saying but agreed they were arguing. That, along with the fact that Jimmy lives with you, Sally, and I know you keep all kinds of medical supplies at home, including syringes— well, I had no choice but to bring him in."

"*What?*" we all said, and then started shouting our objections at once until the noise level started attracting dogs.

"Quiet down, everyone, so Augie can hopefully explain himself." I called the room to order.

"Those syringes are for Joe's allergies. Are you kidding me, Augie?" Sally was incredulous.

"I'm afraid this is no joke and I have a warrant to search your home. We're parked just in front, if you'll be kind enough to open up for us."

* * *

We all flew out of Peggy's house to look up the street.

"So much for kicking curse's' butts," Sally said.

"This has nothing to do with a curse," I said. "It was suggested that the fish stuffed with heroin came from in or around Nicaragua, and we now know the poison that killed Jonas most likely came from Columbia."

"So?" Aimee asked.

"I'm afraid these shipments could be tied to the drug cartel and Jonas may have stumbled on to what was going on. We'd better steer clear if we know what's good for us."

"What about Jimmy?" Sally asked in a scared whisper.

"He's probably safest in jail for the time being," Peggy replied.

"At least until we find out who killed Jonas," I said.

"But how are we going to do that? We can't go messing with drug dealers!" Aimee was tearing up.

"We will *appear* to have lost interest, but that doesn't mean we can't work on the case in other ways. Everybody in?"

"No. This isn't right, and I don't want to put you girls in danger. This is a family matter and Joe and I should be the ones—alone—to deal with it."

This was more than Sally had said all day.

"Is that what we do, ladies? When someone is in trouble, do we walk away and let them sort it out for themselves?" Peggy asked.

"Not in my neck of the woods we don't," said Mary Ann.

"Nuh-uh," said Aimee between sobs.

"Then I ask again," I said, looking at Sally. "Everybody in?"

I put my hand out, and each girl, including a reluctant Sally, placed hands on top in a pledge of solidarity. "Time for stealth sleuthing."

CHAPTER 10

After numerous phone calls, several mini Wine Clubs and some clandestine meetings, a plan was hatched and ready to be executed. We crouched in the shadows of the Santa Monica airport.

"There must be another way to get in from the back," I whispered as we crept along the side of the north runway.

"I'm really hating this idea," Aimee said, forgetting to whisper.

"Shhh," we all replied.

Sally, Peggy, Aimee and I had figured tonight was as good a night as any to go back and check out Rusty's hangar. With Jimmy arrested and in jail, we hoped that everyone involved with this drug operation would be taking a breather.

We were about to find out how wrong we were.

It was around eleven and the small airport was closed to air traffic. It had a peaceful feel to it, the few navigation lights that were left on casting a warm glow over the open space. Up here, we could really feel the ocean breeze, and if it hadn't been a bit foggy, we'd have been able to see the pier lights on the ocean. Technically, we weren't breaking and entering because there are plenty of open spaces around the field for gaining access. Now, if we found the hangar locked, that would be another story . . .

We'd made a stop at our local sports store earlier in the day and procured headlamps from the camping department. We thought we looked pretty darn cool, even though Peggy chose to wear hers around her neck. Suddenly, we heard a swooshing noise overhead and froze in our tracks. We watched a peregrine falcon descend on a field rabbit crossing the runway and scoop the creature up in its impressive talons. That got me thinking again about what Charlie might have hit that could also quickly disappear. Falcons hunt at night, so I ruled out that possibility. The answer was there in my brain somewhere.

"Let's keep moving," Sally said. "The sooner we get answers, the sooner we can spring Jimmy."

"We're going to have to figure out how to expose whatever we find. We can't exactly cop to breaking into a hangar," Peggy responded.

"First the problem, then the solution," Sally replied.

"How about an anonymous phone tip?" Aimee offered. "I do them all the time."

We all stopped to think about that for a minute.

"Someone's coming!" I could hear several sets of footsteps coming from not too far behind us. "Turn off your lights, and let's hurry to the hangar, where we can hide. It could be animals or patrol officers; either way, we can't get caught or Jimmy has no hope."

We all broke into a quiet run, and as soon as we reached the north row of buildings, I led them to the hangar Rusty used as his headquarters. We quietly crept toward the back of the cavern, away from any light sources.

"I can't see!" Aimee complained.

"Everybody get behind me," I said. "I have my hand on the outside wall of the hangar. I'm going to follow it along until we reach the back. Sally, hold on to my other hand, and then Aimee, grab Sally's and Peggy, you bring up the rear."

We snaked our way around to the back, and when we turned the corner, something or someone ran straight into me, knocking me and the other three down like bowling pins.

I felt something wet on my face and assumed I was bleeding. Until I heard the sniffing around my ear.

"Bardot?"

I flipped on my headlamp and sure enough, my dog was staring down at me, ears flopping and tail wagging. There was a leash attached to her collar. I pivoted the light so I could see who was attached to the other end.

"Marisol! What are you doing here with Bardot?"

From behind me, I heard rustling and looked to see the girls in various stages of sitting up.

"Bardie needed to go out, I could hear her crying from my house," Marisol explained with authority.

I turned to her, and when the headlamp hit Marisol's face, I noticed she had duct-taped small flashlights to each side of her camo Krispy Kreme Doughnut cap. I stood up.

"First of all, that is *not* her name and you know it. Second, she'd been out just before I left. Third, if, and I mean *if*, she needed to go out, since when do you take her all the way to the airport? At midnight? You were following us, weren't you?"

"Nuh-uh." She shook her head, and the flashlights slipped from their forward position and the lights crossed in front of her. She looked like she had run face-first into a lightsaber war.

"And what is with that ridiculous head thing you have on?"

"I need to be able to see to pick up Bardie's—I mean Bardot's poop."

I gave her the evilest eye I could muster.

"You and I are going to have a long talk when we get home to reestablish new ground rules. And I want my house key back. You girls okay?" I asked the group behind me.

"We're good, Halsey. It seems you took the brunt of the run-in," Peggy said.

Sally took off her lamp and shone it over my face. "Your nose is starting to bruise. I hope it's not broken."

"Geez," I moaned and gently ran my hand over my very tender proboscis.

"Hey, you guys, this door's unlocked!" Aimee had stumbled upon a point of entry into the hangar.

"Marisol, you and Bardot stay right where you are, I mean it! Keep watch and let us know if you hear anyone coming. Understand?"

"English is my first language, and what I don't understand is why you're so cranky. It's past your bedtime, isn't it?"

I made a move toward her, and Sally pulled me back to the hangar door.

Once we were inside, I turned on a more powerful flashlight I'd been carrying in my backpack and handed a second one to Peggy.

"Shall we each check a corner?" Peggy asked. "Aimee, come with me."

I nodded, and Sally and I went toward the area where I'd visited Rusty's workspace with Jack.

"It looks just like it did the other day," I whispered to Sally. I slowly let the light scroll along the corner walls. Sally, impatient to find something, used her headlamp to go over the shelves above the work desk. Meanwhile, I picked through a metal bucket that held rolled-up plans.

"Wait a minute," I said, trying to keep the paper I'd opened from curling back into itself. "Sally, can you hand me that big wrench over there?"

I anchored one end in place and held the other side.

"Don't tell me you actually know what you're looking at, Halsey. If you're that smart, I'm going to have to have an honor-student bumper sticker made with your name on it!"

"Keep your voices down," we heard Peggy admonish.

"I couldn't build a plane from this, but some of the parts sound familiar."

I ran my light over the plan all the way to the bottom right corner, where the legend was.

"Crapola! Well, we know Rusty's a liar."

"How?" Sally peered over my shoulder.

"These are plans for a Pietenpol Air Camper. It says so right here."

"Oh-kay?"

"I specifically asked him about one, and he said he didn't know what I was talking about."

"Oh. I was hoping for something more damning."

"We'll find it, Sally."

"Maybe we already have," said Peggy, joining us.

"Yes! What have you got?" Sally jumped up and down, creating an eerie echo throughout the chamber.

"Check this out," Aimee said, showing us an open book. "This is a *Sunset Western Garden Book* from 1979. We found it under a big, smashed ice cooler."

"And? Is this the nail in Rusty's coffin?" Sally was clearly agitated.

"This page was bookmarked," Peggy said, taking the book from Aimee.

It was part of the B section in the alphabetized western plant encyclopedia.

"He was interested in growing Brussels sprouts? So what?"

I took a closer look at the two pages.

"Look at this listing, Sally," Peggy continued. "'Brugmansia.' It says they have 'tubular' flowers and are known as 'angels trumpet.' Flowers and seeds are poisonous if eaten. Other common names are almizclillo, baumdatura, borrachera,' and it goes on from there. That seems like more than a coincidence."

I studied the inset photo of the plant. It looked familiar, but I couldn't place it.

"This book has probably been lying here since 1979, long before Rusty would have started working here." Sally was emphatically advocating for the devil.

"True, but look what the page was marked with." I held up the item.

"It's a business card from Spitfire Grill," Aimee declared.

"And?"

"And Sally, in 1979 that coffee shop was called the Kitty Hawk. It didn't become the Spitfire Grill until 1991. Haven't you ever read the history on their menus?"

"So, even if the book is old, the bookmark was placed in the last twenty-five years."

"Correct, Peggy, but I bet we can narrow it down even more by checking with the owners. They can tell us if this is the current logo they use, and if not, when it was discontinued." I really felt like we had a solid lead.

"Okay, I feel better," Sally admitted. "But we should skedaddle before someone catches us or the curse rears its ugly head."

That was when we heard the sound of the big overhead lights power up.

"Who's in here? This is the police."

"Augie?" I thought I had whispered his name, but it echoed loudly.

"Don't tell me. If you're in here, Halsey, it could be very bad for you."

I motioned with my hand for everyone to leave, pointing to Sally in particular.

Augie added his flashlight to the overhead lights and found us gathered in the dark back corner of the hangar. The only good news was that he seemed to be alone.

"Tsk, tsk, tsk," he said, approaching us.

"This is not at all what it seems, Augie." I was forceful even though I had zip, zero, nada to back up my statement.

"Really? And how do you know what I interpret this little coffee klatch to be?"

"How dare you? We would never get together to drink coffee!" Peggy had been insulted and she was making it known.

"You're right, Augie, I couldn't possibly know. Why don't you tell us what we're doing here?"

"Well, it's pretty clear you are all—very clever, Halsey. You almost got me. You'll have a chance to explain it to me in excruciating detail at the station. Put your hands behind your back. I'm arresting you."

"You're being ridiculous, Augustus. We have every right to be here, and for the same reason you are."

"Aunt Marisol?"

Augustus? Hail, Caesar!

I turned around and saw Marisol and Bardot enter through the back door.

"And you need to tell whoever is in charge of this place that they left the backdoor open and unlocked. You're not the one in charge, are you?"

"No, Auntie."

"Glad to hear it. Now come on. I can hear the chopper starting up. Let's go watch the medevac."

Marisol pranced along the hangar with Bardot toward the runway opening. I quickly caught up to her.

"What was that all about? A medevac?"

"Heard it on my portable scanner. An emergency organ transplant patient is being transported out of here. Could save his life, and people say this airport serves no real purpose anymore? Ha!"

In front of us, sure enough, a helicopter was starting up. And from the east side where we'd entered the runway, an ambulance was driving toward it. The rest of the gang caught up with us.

"Just like we talked about, girls, we are witnessing a lifesaving service from our dear neighborhood airport," I said, both for Augie's and the ladies' benefit.

The ambulance slowed and then stopped about thirty feet from the plane. We watched the paramedics open the back of the vehicle and then pull out a stretcher. They then adjusted it so the patient was in a seated position. The blades were really stirring up the air, so all of us girls huddled together. I took control of Bardot's leash. She seemed to think she was going on this mission and I had to explain otherwise.

When they wheeled the patient past us, I gasped. It was a kid. He couldn't have been more than seventeen or eighteen. I felt my eyes water.

We watched as they loaded him into the belly of the copter facing backward, and all of us waved and blew kisses. I swear, I saw him smile. Once he was safely inside, the medics helped close the door and then joined us to watch the takeoff. Moments later, with the rotors at full speed, it lifted up, and once it reached sufficient altitude, it took off.

"Godspeed, young man," I said.

"And good night, Augustus," Peggy added as we walked off.

CHAPTER 11

I was startled awake by a rap on my bedroom window that was made scarier when I realized that meant someone was in my backyard. Bardot lifted her head up for a quick sniff and then dropped it back down and resumed snoring. This signaled to me that I was safe from any imminent danger. The rapping started again, and I had no choice but to see who it was.

I parted the drapes a few inches and recoiled in shock. I wondered if I was having a nightmare. I'd only been asleep for a few hours after our midnight airport run.

"Go away!"

I returned to my slumber-land cocoon and pulled the covers over my head. That's when I heard the window slide open.

"You going to sleep all day?"

"Maybe. Go away, Marisol."

"That's how you talk to somebody who saved your bacon last night?"

She had a point, damn her.

I looked at my phone and saw it was already nine-thirty.

"What's up?" I asked Marisol, swinging my legs over the edge of the bed. I noticed that none of this held any interest to Bardot, but with her eyes closed, she quickly slid into the warm space I had just vacated in the bed.

If they ever do a remake of the movie Wait Until Dark *with an all-dog cast, I'll have to audition her.*

I threw on one of Jack's shirts and padded my way into the living room and out the French doors to the back.

"Morning, Marisol." I actually did owe her and figured I'd better start paying it off right away. Civility counts, right?

"That's what you're going to wear? Oh well, no one's going to be looking at you anyway. Get your car keys. We've got to go."

"Whoa, whoa, slow down there, slick. You just dragged me out of bed. I haven't had a chance to ponder my sartorial elegance for the day. And just where do you think I'm going to drive you at this hour?"

"You do realize kids have been in school for almost two hours already? And rush hour's over and some people are already thinking about lunch, like me."

I'd like to smack her with a summer sausage right in the kisser.

"Are you going to tell me what you need, Marisol, or not?"

"We."

"We? We what?"

"What *we* need, not just me."

"Okay, tell me what *we* need." I started thinking about a Bloody Mary.

"We need to get going so we can follow Jeb. I saw him get a package from the mail carrier and toss it in his trunk. He went in and got his car keys and he's about to pull out of the driveway."

"Jesus, Mary and God help me, why didn't you say so?"

"I just did."

I ran in the house, grabbed my keys, wallet and a pair of sweats and met Marisol at my car.

"He just drove up the hill," she said, foraging for the peanut butter crackers I sometimes keep in the middle console.

"You eat those in here and make crumbs and you won't live to see your favorite holiday, Halloween."

"Another month."

"What are you talking about? It's only February."

"No, you just got another month added to what you owe me. If I were you, I'd start being nicer to me."

I started humming *The Addams Family* theme song just to keep from driving us off a cliff.

Jeb drove his blue Honda at a reasonable pace and hadn't taken the freeway, so I managed to stay two car lengths behind him. Wherever he was headed, he was in no rush to get there. We were going east on Washington Boulevard.

When I lived in New York, we laughed at the thought of Los Angeles being a city. It just seemed to be a series of suburbs linked by asphalt, with no real history or heart. Since I've moved and spent time here, I've realized just how much of a misconception that is.

The pace and the timing of the lights allowed me the luxury of time to peruse the buildings of the changing neighborhoods. As we progressed in the direction of downtown Los Angeles, I noted that the percentage of new construction to old was rising in favor of the latter. We passed some real historical landmarks. Even Culver City, where we were driving now, was a pleasant mixture of new restaurants, theaters and apartment complexes surrounding the historic lot where Sony Pictures currently reside. Since its incorporation in 1917, Culver City has given birth to such classic movies as *Gone with the Wind*, *The Wizard of Oz*, *Citizen Kane* and *Meet Me in St. Louis*. Desilu Studios was here and thriving in the day, and I could just picture Desi and Lucy driving through the gates in a turquoise and white glimmering convertible.

Marisol distracted me by fiddling with something in her purse. Actually, *laundry bag* was a more appropriate identifier, given its size and expanded bottom.

"What are you doing?"

"I'm setting up my electronics," she replied, not looking up from the task at hand.

"What electronics? You finally send that flip phone to the Smithsonian?"

"Don't make fun of my phone or I'll add another month."

"You don't get to just add months."

"Do too, and it's not my phone I'm working on."

Note to self: next time get a car with a passenger seat Eject button.

She finally pulled a contraption out of her purse that looked kind of like a black plastic ping-pong paddle. She set it on her lap and went back in for another forage. This time, she brought out one of those square batteries.

"Isn't that the same kind of battery you were looking for when we were going to the aquarium?

"Yep. Got a package of six at Costco."

"You go to that place once a week; how can you use up all those bulk items in such a short time?"

"I don't. I go there for the parties."

"What parties?"

"Sometimes Wednesdays, sometimes Thursdays. I have a friend who works there. She calls me when she sees them setting up."

I was beginning to think she'd finally slipped off the edge of the swimming pool and into her own fantasy world when it suddenly dawned on me.

"You mean you have a scout who tells you when the food samples will be given out. You're freeloading."

"I am not, I always pay my way."

"*Ha.*"

"They're the ones offering. It would be rude if I didn't taste their food. I had snow crab legs when I got the batteries."

We were now past Culver City, heading into East LA. If Jeb was going downtown, he was a lot farther south than he needed to be. These neighborhoods have a reputation for gangs and violence, and while I wouldn't walk around here alone at night, I was fascinated with the surroundings going past my window. This was truly a cultural buffet coexisting on the same table. On one side of the street I spotted a party supply store for kids, the Paradise Hotel, which I'm guessing rents by the hour, and the Samosa House for Indian pastries. On the other side was an auto body shop, a place to get hair extensions and, ironically, a salon offering Brazilian waxing. Don't go there.

When we passed the King Farad Mosque and a Baptist missionary, I started humming, "We Are the World."

"Can you believe all these different people are living and working together in one neighborhood?" I asked Marisol. "I am so proud of my city!"

Marisol stuck her index finger into her puffed cheek and pulled it out to make a popping noise.

"You're jaded, that's your problem. Or maybe you're just old."

"Jeb's turning right, you see that?" Marisol shouted.

"I see that, and I heard that; we're only about two feet away from each other, you know? You don't have to yell."

Marisol was back fishing around in her purse and pulled out something resembling a microphone. She opened the base and connected the battery and then screwed the device into the middle of the ping-pong paddle thing. Finally, Marisol extracted a set of headphones from her bag and connected the jack to the device.

"I see you've expanded your spying paraphernalia, I'm guessing this is a remote listening device."

"You're welcome. This way we'll hear everything he says," she replied, and I tried not to think about the distance between my bedroom and her kitchen window.

I still had Jeb in my sights. "It looks like we're heading into Watts."

It occurred to me that I had some living history sitting right next to me.

"What do you remember about the 1965 Watts riots, Marisol?"

"I was just a young girl."

I quickly did the math. *She was old enough to have a driver's license.*

"Were you scared?"

"I just remember being mad that my show kept being interrupted by news. *Bewitched* was my favorite."

Why am I not surprised?

"Then little Augie and a bunch of my family helped serve Thanksgiving dinners one year in Watts. I made some friends, so I continued coming back until I'd had my first baby."

Crap, now she's Mother Teresa. The thought of being nice to her for the rest of my life was killing me.

We'd followed Jeb onto a narrow side street and watched him slow and pull over to the curb. Marisol quickly donned her headphones and fiddled with some dials.

"'Midnight Mercy Mission,'" I read off the sign adorning a two-story concrete building that took up the entire block. A seven-foot wrought-iron fence with some menacing-looking barbs at the top protected the structure from unwanted trouble. But in the middle of the day, the front gates were open, and needy families had lined up to receive sack lunches. Jeb had gotten out of his car and was leaning on his door, watching the scene. He had a warm smile on his face. I pulled in to a space a couple of cars ahead of him.

"Is this the mission you worked at?"

Marisol shook her head.

"But I think I recognize a couple of the staff. I can go talk to them."

I quickly grabbed her sleeve. "Oh no, you don't, at least not while Jeb is here. Our job is to observe. Remember, this could all be nothing."

We watched Jeb go around to the back of his car and open the trunk. He disappeared from view for a second, then shut the trunk door and crossed the street. He was now carrying a package.

"What do you think he has in there, comic books and Green Stamps?" Marisol was snide when she was right, something I would never be . . .

Jeb walked past the line, greeting some of the people along the way, and turned right to go around to the side of the building. I started up the car and did the same along the street.

"Can you hear anything?" I asked Marisol, who looked like she was a sequestered contestant on a seventies quiz show with those big headphones. She ignored me.

"Can you hear anything?!" I shouted this time into the microphone. She jumped a foot into the air.

"I can hear everything, and that hurt. I'm right here. You don't have to shout."

"Didn't I just get finished telling *you* that?"

I leaned into her and pulled one earphone out so I could listen in.

Jeb: *"Sorry I wasn't able to come by sooner, Alice, but the good doctor didn't send me anything for a couple of weeks."*

Alice: *"We're grateful for anything you can provide, dear sir. This is a godsend and will go a long way toward helping the sick children get well. And please thank the doctor for us."*

I watched Jeb hand the envelope to Alice.

"Medicine!" I said a little too loudly, and Marisol jumped again and pulled off the headset. "Jeb must be ordering pills from Mexico and donating them to the mission."

"Looks that way, but why don't they just go directly through the doctor?"

I thought about that. Marisol had a point.

"Unless there really isn't a doctor prescribing the medication. I remember Mary Ann saying Jeb had been a chemist. Maybe he's doing this all by himself."

"Speak of the devil." Marisol pointed to a white car parked up and across the street. The driver-side window was down, and I recognized Mary Ann.

"Get down!" I shoved Marisol's head, and we both ducked below the dashboard.

"Why are we doing this? Did you sneak some wine when I wasn't looking?"

"No! I suspect Mary Ann followed Jeb just like we did. She's a reporter, after all. This is a matter between husband and wife. He's well-meaning, but Jeb's not going about this in the most legal way. We need to let them sort it out. I'm afraid this has nothing to do with Jonas's murder."

As soon as Mary Ann drove away, we did the same. As we headed home, this time on the freeway, I watched Marisol pack away her spy gear. I realized that every time I thought I knew what made her tick, she would introduce some new, surprising aspect of her life into the equation. Some bad, some good. Like serving Thanksgiving meals to the homeless. This made it hard to stay mad at her. Marisol was like a blooming onion, I thought—layers of crispy, golden petals that take on the delicious flavors of the dipping sauces and don't reveal their true impact until you step on the scale the next morning.

"The last digit in Jeb and Mary Ann's house number is seven," she said while playing with my power window.

"So?"

I felt a *Rain Man* moment coming on.

"Sally's last number is one."

I looked at her and she grinned.

"Just sayin'."

See what I mean?

When I got home, I put Bardot on a leash and grabbed a bottle of cold Elyssia Pinot Noir Brut

Cava from the fridge and headed down the street to Sally's house. It was now midafternoon and, as I had guessed, she was reading under a bright red sun umbrella in her backyard.

"I have Bardot and wine. Which do you want first?" I asked Sally after letting myself in through the back gate.

"Oh lord, that's almost as difficult as choosing between red and white."

"Good news then: you can have them both."

I let Bardot run free, and naturally, the pool was her first stop.

"I'll get a couple of glasses and be right back." Sally extracted her long, elegant body from the chaise lounge and gracefully loped into the kitchen.

When she and Joe built the second story, they also expanded the house back to create a library and an outside patio, they shortened their pool, which left them with mostly a ten-foot-deep watering hole. Bardot's favorite depth, and she didn't waste any time diving in.

"I was just reading about the out-of-control, rising cost of drugs set by the pharmaceutical companies in my medical newsletter. Something has to be done about this. It's gotten crazier than a soup sandwich." Sally set down the glasses and I poured. "I mean, how do these people sleep at night?"

"On very expensive sheets, I suspect. It's interesting you brought this up because I have some news for you, but you can't tell anyone else."

"Uh-oh. Now what have you been up to? I'm in enough hot water as it is."

"This is going to give you a clean slate and we

can focus on getting Jimmy off the hook for Jonas's murder."

I proceeded to tell her about our trip to Watts and Jeb's misguided charity work.

"We've got to let this play out between him and Mary Ann. The last thing we want is Augie catching wind of it and making a federal case against Jeb. By the way, whatever came from Augie executing that search warrant for your house?"

"He left with an evidence bag full of goodies, all of which I can account for as being used for valid medical administration. Thank goodness, he didn't bother to extensively look around in the garage, where I stash the real stuff. I think he was put off by Joe's massive book collection lining the walls."

I spat a mouthful of wine back into my glass. I wasn't going to waste it.

"What kind of real stuff?"

"I call it my doomsday kit. This being earthquake country, you just never know if we'll suddenly be cut off from hospitals and in urgent need of medical care. I've been building up the supply for the last fifteen years."

"That makes sense, and it's smart to hide it in a simple, one-story structure. Even in a worst-case scenario, you should be able to get to it. I assume you keep your good wines in there too," I said.

"Damn, I will now!"

We drank in silence for a minute, but I knew Sally knew what I was thinking.

"Okay," she finally said.

"Okay what?" I asked.

"You want me to check to see if anything is missing from my doomsday kit."

"I didn't say—"

"You didn't have to, my friend."

As we rounded the pool to get to the garage, I noticed Bardot had chosen to enjoy the afternoon sun by lounging over the water on the diving board. If you look up *hedonism* in the dictionary, you'll see a photo of Bardot, along with the definition.

"Try not to breath in the dust. I haven't been back here in years. Careful climbing over Joe's *National Geographic* collection."

The floor-to-ceiling, simple shelves sagged under the weight of books arranged by some intricate subject system. You'd pass a section with every paperback Ian Fleming James Bond novel, flanked by a foray into rare and extinct beetles of the insect world. Historical religions led into theories of evolution, and then we-are-not-alone and Area 51 reference books and periodicals. I've always admired Joe's intricate mind, and this offered me a broad tour of some of its wings.

I heard Sally let out a deep gasp.

"What is it?" I asked, rushing back to her.

She was looking into a metal and black case on wheels. The top was open, as were four slide-out drawers, each containing vials, first aid supplies, syringes and pill bottles. Her hand was on the third drawer from the bottom, beside a clearly empty compartment.

"I hate to ask; do you know what's missing?"

She dragged her index finger along the underside of her nose, trying to suppress tears, and nodded.

"I had two vials of hyoscine in this space."

It didn't immediately register with me, so I continued looking at her and waiting for further elucidation.

"Hyoscine is another name for scopolamine, the drug that killed Jonas."

Coincidence *wasn't the first thought that popped into my mind.*

CHAPTER 12

Sally assured me that she would talk to her husband, Joe, about the missing vials and figure out a way to meet with Jimmy in jail to ask him without the cops listening in. She promised to call me later with what she'd learned. I kept thinking back to how dusty the rear of the garage had been, hinting that the medical case hadn't been opened in a long time—certainly before Jonas was killed. But then again, I was looking at the books and didn't actually see Sally open the case. I just assumed it had the same coat of undisturbed grime on it.

I didn't know what to think, and at this point, all I wanted to do was crawl into bed with Bardot and a bag of Flamin' Hot Cheetos and watch *Fixer Upper* reruns. Which is exactly what I did. When my cell phone rang, I was so engrossed in watching Chip Gaines tear out old kitchen counters that I didn't notice the sun had gone down and my bedroom was dark except for the light coming from the TV.

"Hi Sally," I said, groping for the lamp switch on my side table.

"Guess again," I heard a male voice say back to me.

"Jack?"

"The one and only, and your thinking-about-almost-betrothed."

I sighed and then quickly explained to Jack that it had nothing to do with what he had just said. I told him about my afternoon.

"So, you're waiting for Sally to call to confirm that Jimmy had nothing to do with those missing vials? What are you doing right now?"

The moment of truth. Do I confess to my fried, bright red, salty snack indulgence?

"I'm doing some work on the Coast Guard's site, trying to keep my mind off things."

What? It's a white lie, and a little one at that.

"Okay, I'll let you get back to it, but I wanted you to know I'm conducting a seminar in San Diego tomorrow for CARA, and they've agreed to let me take one of their planes. I remember you saying you needed to talk to some people at Montgomery Airport. That's where I'll be flying."

I sat up in bed, spilling Cheetos in the process. Bardot dove in and snarfed one before I could stop her. I watched her eyes grow wide open and then turn watery as her taste buds registered the chili-spiced-encrusted lumpy log of goodness.

"Jack, that's fantastic and exactly the lead I

need. Do you have room for me to bring Peggy and Sally along?"

"Yes, but no more than that. I remember the last time I was fooled into taking the entire Rose Avenue Wine Club for a midnight flight."

"Just the three of us, I swear."

"Okay, babe, I'll have a couple of dogs with me, so let's meet at the airport observation deck at nine-thirty tomorrow morning."

"Perfect! Love you, my almost betrothed."

"Love you back. Don't work too much longer. You've got a big day tomorrow."

"I won't, I promise."

What? I said I won't, and that's not lying.

After I called Peggy and left a message for Sally, I dropped off into a deep sleep. I'm sure a bag of Cheetos and a glass of wine were a contributing factor, as I vaguely remember dreaming I'd witnessed a murder, but every time I tried to tell someone, I couldn't get the words to come out. I would scream the killer's name in my head, but on the outside, all I could do was smile. I awoke in a cold sweat that didn't dissipate when I saw there were no messages or texts from Sally.

It was nine already and I had to hustle. Watching Bardot munch her kibble, it dawned on me that I'd be gone all day, which presented the issue of what to do with her. If I asked Marisol to hang out with her and take her for a walk, she'd no doubt worm out of me the plans for the day. And Jack was adamant about the number of people he would let on the plane. Then again, if Sally wasn't coming . . .

In the end, I decided bringing Bardot along was the best choice all the way around. I dressed quickly and grabbed my makeup bag, figuring I could do that when we were in the air. I saw Peggy waiting by my car, but there was no sign of Sally.

"Where are you going with Bardie?" I heard a voice ask from across the lawn.

Busted.

"Nowhere good. You'd hate it," I said to Marisol, who was leaning on her broom in her driveway, trying to make the pretense of being a meticulous homeowner.

"How do you know I wouldn't like it when you haven't asked me?"

"I just know." I loaded Bardot into the back and Peggy got in the passenger seat. When I went around to the driver's side, Marisol stood in front of the door, blocking my entry.

I must remember to get a DNA sample from her to send to SETI for testing, because she's certainly extraterrestrial and I may even have to concede the intelligence *part.*

"You need to move," I said to her.

"I hope I'm not late," Sally said, loping up the sidewalk. "I didn't get your message until this morning. Of course I want to fly to San Diego with you and Peggy and Jack and go to that restaurant!"

Sally hopped into the backseat and Marisol was distracted just long enough for me to get behind the wheel. I've never been more thankful for automatic locks. We pulled out under a fire-breathing stare from Marisol.

"Nowhere good, my bony butt," she yelled at me.

As we got onto Rose Avenue, I rolled down my window. "I'll bring you back a turkey burger."

"I want my fish back," she replied.

Taking off from the Santa Monica airport just never gets old. You lift off heading west, and in about a minute, you're flying over the ocean. Depending on your flight plan, you head north or south from there. We'd been having some Santa Ana winds, the ones that blow from the desert to the shore and can cause fires and wreck all sorts of havoc on anything in its way. But today, they were gone, and we had a bright blue, cloudless sky. When we had leveled off, I pulled out my makeup. Having lived in New York City, where everyone is always rushing everywhere, I'd gotten very adept at knowing exactly where my eyelashes were and how to wield that magic black wand on them even in the bumpiest of cab rides.

I'd sat in the copilot's seat for takeoff. I could feel Jack staring at me.

"What? You act like you've never seen me put on makeup before."

"It's a show I never tire of, but the orange—is that a new thing? Some spring fashion trend?"

I had no idea what he was talking about until I looked in to my small hand mirror to apply the mascara. Indeed, the fingertips of both my hands were glowing with a slightly muted vermilion color. It looked like I'd been thumb wrestling with E. T. all night. I wasn't about to tell Jack that I had in fact been feasting on a bacchanalian buffet of Cheetos.

"This? No. Marisol is thinking of painting her house and we were looking at colors."

"She's leaning toward that? What's next? Farm animals?"

I laughed. "I set her straight. I'm going back to talk to Sally. She never called me last night."

"Okay. We've got about twenty-five more minutes in the air before I start my descent."

"Aye, aye, Captain."

"There she is," Sally said when I joined them. "I was just telling Peggy about the missing vials. I didn't call you last night because Joe advised me not to ask Jimmy about it over the jailhouse phone, and it was too late for me to go there to ask him in person. Joe said he never even knew I had a stocked medical bag in the garage."

"It would sure be odd for Jimmy to just come upon it," Peggy chimed in. "I've seen that place and its contents. It doesn't exactly invite you to spend some time and browse."

"That's for sure," I agreed. "Sally, not that I think this, but is there any way Jimmy could have overheard you talking to someone about the bag? I'm just trying to cover all the bases and stay ahead of the cops."

"Trust me, I was up most of the night wondering the same thing. This whole situation makes me sick to my stomach. But I can't think of anyone or anytime I may have talked about the supply while Jimmy was in earshot. I know how bad this looks."

"It's only circumstantial, and we need to sit on it

for as long as we can." Peggy put a fine point on it. "And when you do get in to see Jimmy and it's safe to talk, ask him as well about an argument with Jonas that some of the guys claim to have overheard."

"That's the other thing: Jimmy hates confrontation. That's why his ex-wife ran circles around him. I've never seen him pick a fight with anyone, let alone a fellow he'd just met."

"Duly noted, Sally."

"You ladies strap in now. We're about seven minutes out," Jack said over the intercom.

"Aye, aye, Captain," all three of us replied.

The Montgomery-Gibbs Airport is a bit larger than our Santa Monica one but has the same local, relaxed feel. Jack taxied us to the restaurant where we had planned to meet Charlie and then went on his way. We agreed to meet back at the pilot's lounge in a few hours.

I wasn't sure what sort of reception Bardot would get at the Casa Machado Restaurant, but in the worst case, we'd take turns eating and trying to get information out of the waitstaff.

Unlike the Spitfire Grill, this restaurant is situated right on the side of the runway so that while you're dipping a chip, you can also watch a small plane go nose and wheels up. Upon entering, we found ourselves in an environment of old-world Mexico with brick-lined archways into the various rooms, decorative murals, lots of wrought iron and ancient pottery. Homage is paid to the restaurant's location by colorful model airplanes suspended from the ceiling. It was a little early for the lunch crowd and the long Spanish-tiled bar that would be brimming at happy hour with enthusiastic imbibers was currently empty.

"Hi. Three for breakfast or lunch? Or is it three and a half?" said the hostess, noticing Bardot.

"Hi. Is there a place where we can sit with her? If not, I'll wait outside," I offered.

"Technically, we don't allow dogs, but we have a patio and this is a slow weekday, so follow me."

"Thanks so much. My dog, Bardot, thanks you as well."

Bardot immediately wagged her tail. This was the kind of welcome she expected from fine dining establishments.

"Charlie just texted me. He's about ten minutes away," Peggy announced.

"So, there will be four of us," I said, "and a half."

"Great. I'm Chloe and I'll also be your server today. Can I start you off with some guacamole and margaritas?"

We gave one another a guilty look until, finally, Peggy made the decision for us. "I'd like an ice tea, and chips and salsa should be fine for right now."

"You're no fun when you're spying," I said to her after Chloe left.

"We need to stay focused. The stakes are even higher now," Peggy said while looking at Sally, who was uncharacteristically quiet. Again.

Sally had her arms crossed tightly around her chest and her shoulders were slumped giving away her somber mood.

"Okay, how should we play this?"

"Let's have Charlie broach the subject when he

gets here. He has a seemingly innocent reason to ask about the delivery and the waiter that brought it to his plane. Plus, Chloe looks like the typical blond California girl, something Charlie never tires of eyeing."

"That scoundrel!" I replied.

"This gentleman claims he belongs with you. I can shoo him away if that isn't the case," Chloe teased, bringing our drinks with Charlie in tow.

"We can't seem to shake him, so he might as well sit down," Peggy said when Charlie leaned in to kiss her.

When Chloe had placed the last glass on the table, I saw there was still one item left on her tray.

"Don't think I'd forget about you, darling Bardot." Chloe pulled a cloth napkin from the waistband of her jeans and laid it on the floor, then placed a bowl of water on top of it. Bardot melted like ice cream in the Mojave and licked Chloe's face. "I'll give you a few minutes to look at the menu," she said.

"Don't even think I'm going to order anything for you to eat," I said to Bardot. "You had a nice breakfast and you know what Mexican food does to you. We have to fly back in a confined space."

"TMI," Sally said.

"I was saying you should be the one to ask about the origin of the delivery you made from here. Don't mention the contents; say you're just checking on who it came from and who it was going to. Be charming. You remember how to do that, Charlie, don't you?"

Wow, Peggy was on the case.

"This old geezer still has some skip in his step, especially around the fairer sex. I've got this." Charlie winked.

He was going to enjoy this. We studied our menus for a moment. My eye caught an item described as *White Fish Ensalada* and figured I could use this to ask some questions of my own.

"Has everyone decided?" Chloe had returned.

I waited for everyone else to order first and then asked, "This white fish salad sounds yummy. Can you tell me what kind of fish it's served with? Is it caught locally?"

"I'll have to check with the kitchen to see what they are making today, and what about the pup? A *perro caliente*, perhaps?"

"Oh, thanks, but no hot dogs for her."

Sour, garlicky breath does not make for an endearing dog.

"You look familiar," Charlie said to Chloe. "I fly out and back in to here every couple of weeks, but this is my first time eating at this restaurant."

"I've been working here for almost four years now. Maybe you came in here for a drink one night and saw me?"

"I don't think so, but I have flown packages and coolers from this restaurant up to Santa Monica. Perhaps you brought one to my plane?"

"You mean food? Maybe catering? I've never been involved with that."

"The last shipment actually contained frozen fish. A cooler was brought to my plane just before takeoff. The guy had on a Casa Machado shirt. Do you guys also have a place near Mar Vista or Santa Monica?"

"I don't think so, at least not that I've heard. We did have a busboy who was fired a couple of weeks ago. They suspected and finally caught him stealing food and supplies. He was always trying to scam something from someone. Maybe it was him."

"Do you know how we can get in touch with him?" I asked, and probably shouldn't have.

"No. Like I said, he was a slippery guy. I'll get your orders in and get back to you about the white fish."

"Might have been one question too many, Halsey. She couldn't get away from us fast enough," Sally said to me.

"I knew it the minute it left my mouth. You think she's keeping something from us or just got spooked by our probing?"

"Could be both or neither. That's what makes this so frustrating. We need to get some real evidence."

"You're right, Peggy," Charlie said. "I'll do all I can on this end. I do know some guys I've heard take up residence on those barstools during happy hour. And I'll keep trying to figure out why this Chloe looks familiar to me."

"I'm afraid our fish shipment hasn't been delivered yet. Would you like to have chicken or shrimp on your salad?" Chloe said, startling us with her abrupt return.

"I'll have the Burrito Ranchero," I replied. There was no use pretending my interest in the fish wasn't entirely gastronomical. Was she simply protecting the restaurant from any unsolicited attention, be-

ing a loyal employee? Or was she covering for someone like the busboy? Or maybe herself?

"I'm so stupid. I blew this whole thing, you guys.
I feel terrible."

"Don't worry about it, Halsey, you were just trying to help me and Jimmy out." Sally patted my
back while staring out at the action on the runway.

"Sally's right," Peggy agreed. "The important
thing is that Chloe's reaction to our questions was
inconsistent with that of someone who had nothing to hide. Where there's smoke, there's fire, and
we're going to have to rely on Charlie to snuff it
out."

"I'm your man," Charlie said with a puffed-out
chest.

We seemed to have run out of conversation
once the food arrived, the place had started to get
busy and Chloe was clearly done with us. We had
to flag down a waiter when we were ready for the
check, and he took care of our payment. As we
stood, Bardot decided she wanted a souvenir and
pulled the napkin out from under her water bowl,
spilling its content all over the tile floor.

"Geez, Bardot," I said, grabbing the cloth from
her and mopping up the water. "We have certainly
worn out our welcome. I think we can leave out
these back stairs," I said to the group, and we made
a hasty retreat.

We passed the hour before we were to meet Jack
by taking a tour of the airport with Charlie in his
golf cart. I kept my eyes peeled for anything suspi-

cious, desperate to remedy the botched interrogation and salvage something from this trip. We were riding along the far perimeter of the airport when I noticed a yellow parasol-wing small plane taxiing down the runway.

"Charlie?" I called from the backseat of the cart.

There was so much ambient noise from the planes and helicopters that he didn't hear me. I tapped him on the shoulder and he drove around the side of a hangar, where the noise was muffled.

"I wanted to ask you about that plane that's taking off, the yellow one. Do you know if Rusty ever flies down here?"

Charlie's eyes followed where I was pointing, but unfortunately, the plane had lifted off and was banking, so we couldn't see the tail numbers.

"It's entirely possible. You think Rusty owns a Pietenpol?"

"I think so, but I'm trying to prove it."

"I can check with the tower later to see if they can identify the plane and its ownership."

"Interesting," Peggy said. "If we can connect this plane to Rusty, we might be able to link it to the one that dive-bombed Halsey. More importantly, it might give us what we need to show Rusty was seen at the airport where the drug shipment originated."

"And maybe tie him to Chloe. What if that's where Charlie had seen her before? Not here, but with Rusty at the Santa Monica airport," I added.

"Now that's a thought." Peggy was adding up the pieces.

"Maybe," Charlie replied.

"That's a lot of ifs and maybes." Sally wasn't ready to jump on the breakthrough bandwagon.

We were all drained. The entire day had been an ordeal, and when I saw my amber-eyed redwood of a man stride over to us, I couldn't resist running into his arms for a good, old-fashioned bear hug.

On the flight home, we all sat mostly in silence. I was up front with Jack, and after I told him about questioning Chloe and pretty much shut down any hope of getting a lead, we had words over me thinking I was a detective. It's been a bone of contention with us since we met. He is concerned for my safety and thinks I should leave solving crimes to the experts. To some extent he's right, and in one instance my sleuthing landed me in jail—and we hadn't spoken for a week. On the other hand, my success rate was two for two, and the Rose Avenue Wine Club had saved a number of innocent people from prison. We'd also stopped a number of seriously guilty people from continuing in their nefarious ways.

My phone vibrated, and I saw it was Shelly from the aquarium.

"Hi Shelly, I was hoping to hear from you. Again, I apologize for any trouble I may have caused you with Bardot."

She chuckled. "That's water under the bridge. By the end of the day, everyone was laughing about it, and now we get asked to see the underwater dog."

"I'm so glad. Hey, I'm here with a few friends

who are also anxious to hear your report. Do you mind if I put you on speaker?"

"No, go right ahead."

Jack handed me the microphone for the intercom and turned it on.

"Okay, Shelly from the aquarium," I said for Sally and Peggy's benefit, "what did the tests on the fish sample say?"

"We identified the species as Parachromis managuensis, or what the locals of Central America call *guapote*. It's a freshwater fish, as I suspected, but you'll want to put air quotes around the word *fresh*. As the name implies, they come from Lake Managua in Nicaragua. They're carnivorous and big-time predators, especially for their size of just about fourteen inches."

"Ugh, they sound like perfect pets."

"Not exactly, Halsey. Now, here's the deal with Lake Managua, affectionately called one of the most contaminated lakes in the world."

Ah, another fan of sarcasm.

"It presents a constant threat but also a temptation for the poor people of Nicaragua. They know it's teeming with fish and they're hungry, but they also know the water they live in is basically a forty-mile-long sewer from years and years of drainage and dumping from the city."

We responded with a chorus of "Ew."

"Still, out of desperation, some of the neediest people of Managua still live around the lake and eat the fish."

"Shelly, this is Jack. Thanks so much for helping us out with this. The results you are giving us are much more specific in terms of location than we ever could have imagined, which is great! Are you confident in the pinpoint of this *guapote* to that specific lake?"

"Hi Jack. I'm very confident based on the DNA testing that was done. But in addition, we have a colleague here who is from Nicaragua. Before Eddy came to work at the aquarium, he worked with a US company and the DEA, acting as a guide through the El Brujo Natural Reserve. He confirmed the analysis and told me these fish, because of their abundance and the reticence of customs people to touch them, are easy to ship out of the country with drugs smuggled inside."

"Sound like we've got one on the hook," I heard Peggy shout from the back.

CHAPTER 13

The long day turned into a long and silent night. Jack still wasn't speaking to me except for essential communication like, "I'm heading home." Bardot was equally nonresponsive after her day of what she no doubt considered shenanigans and hijinks. She raced to the bedroom and sprawled out in the center of the bed and was out like a light. I paced and stewed for a bit, but after a quick nip of Glen Garioch 12 single malt, I joined Bardot in rapturous slumber.

I was woken in the morning by a call from Mary Ann, asking if I'd like to meet her downtown for a tour of the *Los Angeles Times* offices. Of course I jumped at the offer to experience more of my new home's history, and I had a pretty good idea she wanted to talk about Jeb. We agreed to meet at eleven-thirty, with lunch to follow. Little did I know at the time that this would be a working lunch.

I'd been in front of and driven past the *Times* building on several occasions, usually on my way to a concert at Disney Hall, an early morning trip to the flower market or on a very necessary procurement mission for Slippery Shrimp from Yang Chow in Chinatown. Depending on traffic, it can take as little as fifteen minutes to reach downtown or over an hour if there's been an accident. I kept promising myself I'd take a Saturday to go there and become a total tourist, but beach going or murder solving always got in the way.

Located on Times—Mirror Square, the *Los Angeles Times* has resided in this building since it opened in 1935. It's a monumental, grand example of Art Deco architecture as designed by Gordon B. Kaufmann. The outside is adorned with newspaper-style sculptures, a big clock and the words "The Times" etched in the towering limestone façade.

Though I'd seen photos, my breath was still taken away when I entered the ornate Globe Lobby, named for the metal five-and-a-half-foot globe that sits on a pedestal in the center of the rotunda. Ten-foot murals depicting LA's history and that of the newspaper business adorn the surrounding walls. I stood in awe and felt a chill being so close to artist Hugo Ballin's depiction of iconic Los Angeles history. A series showed the process a newspaper undergoes before landing on your doorstep, from a writer working on a typewriter through printing and delivery. Others show scenes from the WPA era, including men working on public buildings, utilities and roads and people in the arts.

"You know, I've been walking through here for over thirty years now and rarely do I stop and do what you're doing now."

I turned in the direction of the voice and saw it was Mary Ann.

"I'm sorry if I'm late, but I had to take this all in. I've learned quite a bit about the history of the Westside and Mar Vista but haven't had a chance yet to explore the beginnings of Los Angeles here."

"Be careful not to say that too loudly. This place is teeming with old men reliving their glory days as Chandler cub reporters. Before you know it, you'll be plying them with roast beef and old-fashioned cocktails for their stories."

She linked arms with me and led me to the elevators. I haven't spent much time with Mary Ann and I couldn't help but notice she was in fine spirits today. Maybe this was due to being in her work environment, or maybe it was from something else. I figured I was about to find out.

"I'm a part-timer now, so I don't have my own office. The *Times* keeps workstations for the floaters, as they call us, and today I was able to snag one by a window with an amazing view."

She giggled with excitement, and that got me laughing. I knew she could be cutthroat when working a story, but her bright eyes and the bounce in her step made this pixie woman easy to underestimate. Think Sally Field and Evelyn Salt combined and you'll get the picture.

As much as I embrace all things digital, I'm still a sucker for the printed word. I realize every morning that the newspaper I'm reading contains stories that were pushed to me almost a day before on my phone, but I still treat them with respect. These people paved the way for me to know the second a Kardashian lands at LAX or which third-world country has just had a coup. So as long as there's a newspaper to be read, I'll buy it.

Mary Ann gave me the nickel tour of her floor and introduced me to the reporters and researchers for the various sections. I immediately recognized the respect and admiration they had for her, and I wondered if roast beef and an old-fashioned would be my price of admission to hear her stories. Certainly worth a try.

"And this is where I call home today. I'm just polishing a piece I've been working on about municipal airports, including, coincidently, ours in Santa Monica. I could be doing this from home, but frankly, I miss the camaraderie around here. Plus, spending too much time with Jeb is exhausting."

"I don't blame you. If I had a view like this from my desk, I'd be here every day too," I said, staring out at the palm trees and City Hall.

"Have a seat, Halsey. I also managed to scrounge up a guest chair, something that's really a premium around here."

I settled in, noticing the very transient feel to Mary Ann's desk. I'd imagined she'd be the kind of office worker to adorn her space with memories and inspiration. A photo with Mayor Tom Bradley, a signed Dodger baseball, maybe a pressed flower from Jeb. But the only personal item on her workstation today was a fob with her car keys.

"I figured you'd enjoy coming here, and I wanted to talk to you alone, which isn't always easy on Rose

Avenue," she began. "I have a confession of sorts to make."

I nodded and figured she needed to experience the catharsis of telling me about Jeb, so I let her continue while subtly letting on that I had no plans to involve the authorities on this matter.

"When I'm not on my laptop for work, Jeb and I share the same computer at home. I hopped on a few days ago to send some links to my nephew, who's getting ready to look at colleges. That's when I saw that Jeb had left an email open on the screen from an organization calling itself Medications Without Borders. Well they should add *Without Prescriptions.* You know me: I had to check these people out. Jeb's heart was in the right place. He'd read about the dire need that missions have in Los Angeles for healing drugs, so he first approached his contacts in the pharmaceutical industry. When that didn't pan out as quickly as he would have liked, he got the idea that, being a chemist, he would make the drugs himself. I guess when I was at work one day there was a small fire in the kitchen, and that scared him off that path. So, he went online. I saw you in Watts that day, so you know how this story ends."

That took me by surprise. Mary Ann really is good; I'll have to remember that for future spy missions.

"First, I want you to know that I would never have told anyone about this, especially the cops. As far as I'm concerned, the matter is between you and Jeb."

She looked at me, expecting me to say more.

"Marisol knows that as well, and as slippery as she can be, she knows how to keep a secret. We have several between us."

"Whew. I can't tell you how relieved I am to hear this, Halsey. Jeb's a good man, he really is . . . it's just that since he's retired, he doesn't know what to do with himself. I would go a little nutty too. I need to keep busy and that's why I still work part-time. The same day he was at the mission, I confronted Jeb. He understood he couldn't go on dispensing medicine that way. We spent the next day sourcing legitimate, regulated organizations and identified some great prospects. He's been interviewing them."

"Perfect. Consider the matter closed. Augie knows he has nothing substantive to tie Sally to that package, so eventually he'll have to let that go. Now, the heroin is another matter, and I was hoping you could help me with that. I suspect once we solve who's dealing these drugs, we'll also know who murdered Jonas."

"Now you're barking up my kind of tree," Mary Ann said, firing up her laptop.

I filled her in on our trip to San Diego and the possible connection to Rusty at our airport. The work she'd been doing for her article on local airports dovetailed well with what I needed. The next thing I knew, it was already one o'clock, and the food Mary Ann had ordered had arrived.

She'd made it clear that no visit to Downtown was complete without feasting on the famous #19 pastrami sandwich from Langer's Deli. I smiled politely, thinking deep down that it couldn't possibly come close to the Reuben from the Carnegie Deli in New York, which I used to need to eat at least once a week. Boy, was I wrong.

"You may want to look away; this isn't going to be pretty," I told Mary Ann as I felt Russian dressing and coleslaw escape the corner of my mouth.

She giggled. "Enjoy it, Halsey. I knew you would."

"Om nom" was about all I could manage to respond.

"Let me try to summarize what I've learned that could have bearing on this case."

Again, all I could do was nod, the combination of soft bread and crunchy crust serving as the perfect platform for savory pastrami and warm, gooey Swiss cheese. I thought that even if I had a glass of wine in front of me, I probably wouldn't stop to take a sip because this was so good. Or not.

"As you know, at general aviation airports, planes aren't searched unless the pilots consent or officials have probable cause warrants. They need enough evidence to show that a crime has been committed. This seldom happens at the stage where small planes are flying within the United States. The place where most of the drug smuggling is detected is at the border—mostly Mexico, in our case—where warrants aren't required for a search."

"So, if the drugs get past the border, they're home free?" I'd finally managed to control my gorging.

"Not necessarily. We have lots of government workers scrutinizing and tracking small-plane activity within the US. They look for anything that stands out, like . . . continuous odd flight routes, passengers and cargo, aircraft type and pilots and owners. It's just that the volume is so high, they have to focus on the bigger operations."

I thought about that for a minute and felt the weight of this impossible task. Maybe it was better just to focus on Jonas's murder and try to clear Jimmy for that alone. But I couldn't shake the nagging feeling that the two were connected.

"Mary Ann, we can now confirm that the drug-stuffed fish found on Charlie's plane came from Lake Managua. Have you run into any intel on Nicaraguan drug smuggling into the US?"

"You better believe it; these guys are some of the worst. They've had to get very inventive on how they bring their narcotics across the border into Mexico. Food has become a popular vehicle."

I stopped munching for a second. "Food?"

"They hide the drugs in tamales, bananas, pastries, chili peppers, you name it. But as the DEA catches on, they find new, inventive ways to hide the contraband. One of the more popular ways now is inside fish."

That got my attention.

"There's the story of a truckload of frozen shark carcasses trying to cross into Mexico. In this case, Marines intercepted the cargo and made the arrest. But this still goes on all the time with smaller conduits. It's a lot easier to smuggle cases of smaller fish past inspectors at a ninety-degree checkpoint at the height of the midday sun. The stench alone puts the guards in very lenient moods."

"That is amazing and very helpful. I suspect some drug cartel from Nicaragua is handling the border and then delivering shipments to their reps in the

US for dispersion and sale. For our purposes, we would need to track down the reps doing this out of Montgomery Airport in San Diego. Any ideas on how we can go about finding these jerks?"

"Hmmm. Let me reach out to some of my sources in the field down there. At the very least, we should be able to shake some trees."

"Thanks, Mary Ann. This has been very enlightening and very fattening. I think I'll walk home."

I spent the next two days getting my house and head in order. I had a feeling the coming weeks were going to be very busy with both my work and trying to close this case and bring Jimmy home. And not long after that was Penelope and Malcolm's wedding! I needed to make sure no dark clouds would be hanging over that joyous occasion.

Sally and I had a subsecret, sequestered Wine Club for two on Friday afternoon, which we do on occasion when we want some time together to vent, whine, cry or just split a bottle between us. Today's elixir was a Paso Robles Chardonnay blend called the Tooth and Nail Fragrant Snare. Perfect for spring, this chilled white reminded me of citrus and tropical flavors. As I reclined on a chaise facing the pool, I mentally transported myself to Bora Bora. Sally was on a similar chaise but looked more like she was going up a steep roller coaster.

"How's Jimmy holding up?" I asked her after we'd both taken a moment to sniff, slurp and gulp.

"Not good. He gets more despondent as each

day passes and he's still in jail. Joe and I finally hired a lawyer for him. Jimmy is starting over, so he can't afford one. We're all meeting next week, and hopefully, she'll be able to force the police to either put up or shut up. They still haven't produced any new evidence on him."

I filled Sally in on my meeting with Mary Ann. It was tough to see my usually happy and zany friend with the light taken out of her eyes—she's always been Ethel to my Lucy. This constant threat to her family and uncertainty had put her into an almost catatonic state.

I hated to do it, but I had to ask. "Were you able to talk to Jimmy privately about your medicine bag and the missing vials?"

She nodded slowly. "Just like I expected, he had no idea what I was talking about. He'd never even been in the garage. Jimmy told me that Joe kept offering for him to browse his books and grab anything he was interested in, but Jimmy admitted he's never been much of a reader. So now I'm left with the dilemma of whether to tell the police about the missing vials. It could be the lead they need to solve this, but it might also be the final nail in Jimmy's coffin."

"Maybe talk to this lawyer you've hired about it. She must have some insight on situations like this, and you'd be protected under attorney–client privilege."

"That's using your noggin, Halsey."

Sally's mood had brightened the tiniest bit.

"Is this a private swig fest or can anyone join?" Peggy asked, slipping through my back gate.

Bardot quickly ended her sunbathing on the

floating flamingo pool toy and ran over to greet her best buddy.

"Hello, my beautiful girl," she said, and we all smiled back before realizing she meant Bardot.

"Come on in. I'll get another glass. I might as well get another bottle while I'm at it. Sally, fill Peggy in on the latest."

Bardot followed me into the kitchen, hoping this trip was specifically for her benefit. When she saw that wasn't the case, she resorted to slurping up some water from her bowl and spitting it into the food side, in hopes of making a gravy from any remnants stuck on the bottom. This seemed like such an act of desperation that I relented and gave her a carrot.

"This curse is just never going to end," I heard Sally say when I returned.

"How exactly did it end the last time?" I asked.

"I don't remember. Do you?" Peggy looked at Sally.

"I'm not sure. I just remember one day looking out the window and seeing Danny go by on crutches and thinking that things were finally getting back to normal."

"That's it!" Peggy jumped up from the chair and started doing a little dance.

"What's it?" Sally didn't look amused.

"Danny! Danny's your answer!"

"Peggy, maybe you'd better sit down and explain." I could see steam coming from Sally's ears, while Bardot thought this was a practice audition for the Rockettes and got up on her hind legs and hopped around.

"Danny. Danny is the one you used those vials on. You must have forgotten to replace them."

Sally's eyes got wide and then she got up and did a jig. Bardot reignited her routine.

"You're right!" Sally caught my bewildered face and sat back down.

"Remember what we told you? When the curse started, Danny went out surfing in the big swells and broke his kneecap?"

I nodded.

"When he got home from the hospital, he was having problems with nausea from the anesthesia and experiencing balance issues. Peggy was worried and called me. Danny refused to go back to the hospital. That's when I determined that a small infusion of hyoscine would relieve both of those symptoms. I'd completely forgotten!"

"That's a relief. You'll sleep better tonight. And if all they have on Jimmy is a couple of guys hearing an argument with Jonas, his proximity to syringes and maybe an envelope with medicines, your lawyer should be able to get him out on bail in no time." Peggy had given her summation and it was my turn at the podium.

"We know the package with prescription drugs was meant to be sent to Jeb and Mary Ann's house. The addresser had written a one instead of a seven. Although we won't be talking about that, we're going to have to find another way to prove Jimmy's innocence, while protecting Jeb and Mary Ann. That aspect of the bust is now solved in our minds. We can also trust Jimmy had no access or knowledge of the drug that was found to have killed Jonas. So we know that should clear him once and for all."

"Praise the lord and pass the bacon!" Sally was back.

"We just need enough evidence to make a case," I half-whispered, hoping not to douse Sally's ebullience.

"Unfortunately," Peggy said, raining on our parade, "this means we still have the same thorny crimes to solve: who is smuggling heroin into our airport and who killed Jonas?"

"Correct," I said. "We need to turn up the heat on our investigation, and I may have an idea how."

CHAPTER 14

I assigned myself the task of really understanding the Devil's Breath deadly toxin that had killed Jonas. Augie said it was common in Colombia but hadn't mentioned Nicaragua. Was it grown there too, this borrachero tree? What was the difference in how it was extracted and processed versus the stuff used in hospitals? I gave Bardot a bone stuffed with frozen peanut butter to keep her occupied and sat down at my computer.

A general keyword search returned general links, nothing that was going to help me. I'm a visual person, so when in doubt, I make a schematic of the problem. For this one, I focused on all the possible origins of Devil's Breath the killer could have had access to. Underneath, I added the names of the people I thought could have used each of the methods. When I was finished, this was the result:

Source: Colombia
the borrachero tree
Method:
Seeds are extracted, powdered and chemically processed to
be turned into burandanga, which is similar to scopolamine.
Possible Suspects:
None with clear links to Colombia.

Source: Nicaragua
The borrachero tree is not prevalent due to rabid deforestation from decades of cocaine processing.
Method:
Smuggled from Colombia?
Possible Suspects:
Because fish with heroin came from Managua, Rusty, Chloe, an unknown dealer at Montgomery Airport or
possibly the owners of the Casa Machado restaurant?

And then my research brought this exercise a lot closer to home. I was hyperventilating as I finished my chart.

Source: Local
the angel's trumpet tree
A species of brugmansia, same as the borrachero tree
Method:
Same as in Colombia
Possible Suspects:

Rusty, Britt, love triangle with Jonas?
Or, SODDI*

*some other dude did it

I nearly jumped out of my skin when my cell rang. It was Peggy.

"You're going to need some very fine wine to thank me for what I am about to tell you," she said.

"That can be arranged, Peggy, and I can reciprocate with a juicy discovery of my own."

"You are also going to have to come up with something very special for Charlie. He did all the work."

"Stop with the suspense already! I'm bursting, Peggy."

"Okay. Charlie's cronies had quite a bit to say about our server, Miss Chloe. You saw her; she's just one cup size away from being a blond bombshell."

"Anyone can be blond."

"Well, this blonde has left a trail of male suitors in her wake. She seems to easily fall madly in love and just as easily kick them to the curb. Often, the affairs end with a knock-down, drag-out in that bar after happy hour."

"I'm disappointed but not surprised. So, she's a man-eater who isn't exactly a gateway to a heroin dealer."

"Unless her current man just happens to be from Nicaragua."

Peggy heard me suck in my breath and laughed.

"His name's Oscar Sandoval. Not sure how they

met, but he's been her steady for quite a while now."

"Does he also work at the restaurant? Maybe he was the guy in the Casa Machado shirt that brought the fish to Charlie's plane."

"That would be a long shot. He could have gotten the shirt from somewhere, I guess, but he isn't an employee. Some of the guys heard he owns a nightclub in the Gaslamp Quarter. They think he's got money to throw around. Maybe that's why Chloe has held on to him."

"The money could also easily be the result of drug dealing. We need to get the name of that nightclub. It might necessitate another trip south."

"Will do. Now that I have a name, I've gotten my CIA buddies to do some recon for me. I should have more in a day or so. Pretty good, huh? Now you, Halsey."

Was this the "other dude"? I wondered. The answers were rattling around in my brain somewhere. Maybe I should stand on my head.

"You still there, Halsey? Quid pro quo, now."

"Yes, I'm here, Peggy, and I don't know if what I have to tell you helps or hinders our investigation."

"It's gotta help. You just need some fresh brain cells to ponder it."

"I hope so."

I explained to her about the chart I'd been working on. "Just by chance, I thought I'd see if this Devil's Breath could be grown in Southern California. I'm no botanist, but there does appear to be a species of that tree that grows in abundance all around us. It's called Angel's Trumpet."

"You mean those large bushes with the upside-down, elongated white lilies?"

I laughed. "Those are the ones."

"We keep turning over that same rock. Are the drugs and Jonas's murder separate crimes or not?"

"I know, Peggy, and there's only one person who can tell us that."

"This Oscar guy? I'm guessing he's not going to be effusive with confessions."

"No: Jonas."

"Apart from the obvious, Halsey, how do you propose we do that?"

"We need to walk a day in Jonas's shoes."

"Meaning?"

"Meaning we have to see where he worked, where he lived, who he hung out with, what he ate, the whole nine."

"You're right, but how do we get access to all that?"

"We use our two secret weapons: Marisol and Jack."

If I can convince Jack to come over to the dark, detective side . . .

The big event of the next day should have been viewing the rare solar eclipse. The Wine Club had been preparing for weeks. We'd gotten the special viewing glasses, argued and finally agreed on a menu and set the location. The only teeny, tiny snag was that the best time for us to see this spectacle was at ten in the morning. This limited our options. Somewhat.

We gathered on the bleachers at the Little League field on top of the hill. I noted that everyone was sporting some sort of solar-themed article of clothing; Aimee chose to paint yellow sunbursts on her rosy cheeks. The fare was simple: mimosas, blueberry muffins, fruit salad, and Peggy brought PB&J sammies. I left Bardot at home. I couldn't find any doggles, and there would be no stopping her from staring up in the direction we were looking. Because it was still morning, she didn't seem to mind a bit and unmade my bed and crawled back in.

The guys were invited, and for once, Jack could break free at that hour and join in the fun. We'd declared a truce, and as I always say, *There's nothing like an eclipse to bring out your romantic side.* Or was that an éclair?

"Halsey, I want to thank you," Jeb said, pulling me aside. He was a big guy but gentle. He kind of reminded me of Big Daddy in the Charmin commercials.

"For what, Jeb?"

"Mary Ann told me about your visit to her office and your conversation. My hide is already stinging from my stupidity in how I got those pills. Believe me, Mary Ann will never let me forget it. But if the police had been involved, it would have put pain and stress on her, which would have broken my heart. I've been working with the mission for years, and since retiring, I had some time freed up and wanted to really make a difference."

"Which is exactly what Mary Ann said, and even if she hadn't, I had no intention of interfering. She knew what you were up to and I knew you'd both work things out so you could continue doing your charitable work. Plus, that's an awfully large heart to break. We'd be picking up the pieces for weeks."

Jeb let out a roar of a laugh.

"Cheers, everyone," Peggy toasted as the gang settled down on the bleachers.

We took a group selfie with our crazy glasses on.

"Take it again; you were missing someone," said a voice from under the bleachers.

"Who said that?" Aimee asked.

"Me."

Suddenly, a head popped up in the gap between two tiers. It was Marisol, and she was wearing her safety glasses, as well as the wraparound dark specs she got after having cataract surgery. I wondered how she'd been able to see anything. She must have used her sense of smell to find her way up here.

"Marisol, come around the front and I'll help you up." Jack was ever the gentleman.

Marisol was still trying for the direct, vertical ascent, and we all ended up pulling her through the space between the seats.

"Oh, orange juice," she said, grabbing a flute and taking a big gulp.

She followed it with a loud hiccup. I figured Jack would be carrying her home. She had no idea the juice in her glass wasn't all juice. But she was enjoying herself, probably thinking she was fulfilling one of her mayorly duties of mingling with her constituents on such a momentous occasion. Sometimes, rare times, Marisol just makes me smile.

"Where's Sally?" I asked, noticing she hadn't yet graced our presence.

"I saw her earlier when I went to get the paper," Aimee told us. "She and Joe were just pulling out of their driveway. I waved, but they seemed to be in a hurry and didn't stop to talk."

"I'll bet they were going to meet with the lawyer they've hired to clear Jimmy. I certainly hope this finally closes that chapter on him." I looked up to the heavens for support and noticed the eclipse had started. Meanwhile, Marisol had a sudden insatiable case of the munchies. She'd pretty much cleaned Peggy out of her sandwiches. She was now busy picking the bananas out of the fruit salad and eating them.

"Sorry we're late, but look what the cat dragged along." Sally grinned and hugged Jimmy.

"Yay," we all cheered.

"Come join us. We've got mimosas and," Mary Ann surveyed what was left of the spread, "and more mimosas." She giggled.

Jimmy had clearly lost weight, but he still had that same bright smile that runs in the family.

"Hey, I like your taste in hats," Jeb said, shaking Jimmy's hand. They were both sporting canvas Australian bush hats. "I hope now we can schedule that lunch we've been talking about and catch a Cubs game."

"Where's Joe?" I asked, giving Jimmy and Sally hugs.

"He had a lecture at eleven, so we dropped him off at the university. We're all just so relieved. Our lawyer had Jimmy out in fifteen minutes. He'll be kept under surveillance, but there's just no real evidence."

Either way, I thought. As long as there's a chance

one found clue could be misinterpreted and lead them back to Jimmy, the fat lady hasn't sung. But I was so happy with the joy on Sally's face, I kept my thoughts to myself.

More neighbors had begun gathering on the hill, unloading chairs and snacks from the trunks of their cars and doing the cocktail party mingle.

"Hey, there's my friend," Marisol shouted, standing up on the bench and pointing.

Jack quickly swooped in and grabbed her by the waist to steady her. That little bit of bubbly had clearly gone to her head.

"Where, honey?" Aimee joined her on the bench and swung an arm around her for protection.

"There, that's Joan, Rusty's mom. She works at the post office."

That got my attention, and I was soon standing on the bench with them. Sure enough, Rusty was with her, although by the slump of his shoulders, he didn't appear to be very happy about it.

"Joan! Over here. We've got orange juice!" Marisol's shout was more like a cackle.

The sun was now almost halfway covered, and it cast an otherworldly yellow glow in the sky. Marisol continued to holler and jump up and down; I was so afraid of her falling and breaking her neck, I told her that I'd run over and invite them to join us. It would also give me an opportunity to size up Rusty some more. When I looked back to where they'd been standing, I noticed the spot was now empty. I climbed up to the very top bench and stood on it to scan the field. Their car was still here, so they had to be too.

"You see them?" Marisol was getting impatient and on my nerves.

"Still looking."

Suddenly, a bright yellow flash went by overhead, and when I leaned backward to follow it, I felt my feet slip. The next thing I knew was that I could see the dark sky, and just below it my feet. I braced and landed unevenly with a thud on what felt like two logs. For a moment, I couldn't see or feel anything.

"Are you all right?" I heard a voice I didn't immediately recognize.

I slowly opened my eyes and felt myself being gently lowered, and then I felt the ground on my back. I registered that I was looking directly into Rusty's eyes.

"What? What happened?" I started doing a mental inventory of my body parts, checking for damage.

"You fell, honey." I saw Jack's face come into view. "You were spooked by that damn Pietenpol flying overhead. Anything hurt?" He placed his big hand under my head to prop it up.

"I don't think so." I looked at Rusty. "You caught me?"

He nodded.

"Thanks, man. I owe you big time." Jack shook his hand.

"Gotta go," Rusty replied.

"Don't forget your mama," Marisol shouted to him, "unless you're going to get more orange juice and come right back."

"We've got to find out who was flying that plane so low. That's the second time Halsey has barely escaped getting seriously injured. I'm calling the airport."

I was still stunned but pleased to see that Jack was taking this investigation seriously. But if that plane didn't land at the airport, we'd still be in the dark; even more so, because this time we couldn't suspect Rusty. Also, I needed to keep Jack thinking about solving this rather than seeing it again as dangerous.

"Jack, go for it. I know you can trace that plane."

I tell Bardot all the time not to be a suck-up, but sometimes . . .

Later, at my house, we all gathered in the living room to talk about what had just happened.

"One thing's for sure, Rusty wasn't flying that plane. Did anyone get a look at the pilot?" Peggy was circling the wagons.

They all shook their heads. I was sitting up, but my equilibrium was still a bit off and Sally was checking my blood pressure.

"It was the perfect time for a flyover. We all had glasses on and were focused on the sun. I wish I'd had the presence of mind to register the tail numbers, but all I got were the last two—a zero and a five." Jack entered from the kitchen and placed a cup of tea, just the way I like it, on the end table.

For that he got a kiss. *This kind of protection I'll take all day long.*

"I must scoot, babe, but I'll call to check in on you in a couple of hours. I'm also going to stop by the airport to see if I can get an ID on that plane from the partial I have."

"Actually, and this is for all of you," I started, "Peggy and I thought we needed to turn our attention to Jonas. If we can paint a picture of who he was, what he did, and what he knew, we should be able to identify his killer."

"Great idea. I'm off. I'll dig into that when I'm at the airport as well. Love you."

Jack left, and Aimee stood.

"I've got to get to the shop. We have a birthday party this afternoon," Aimee informed us. "But I've gotten to know Britt a little bit. I'll see what she has to say about Jonas."

"Be subtle," Sally warned, and I felt a pang of guilt again for my pushiness in San Diego. If only I had stuck to superficial questions with Chloe.

"Aren't I always subtle?" She grinned, and her sunburst-painted cheeks inflated.

"I'm afraid I won't be much help. I hardly knew the guy." Jeb got up to leave as well.

Jimmy had gone straight home. "That just leaves us girls," I said.

As if that was a clue, cushions were tossed on the floor, chairs were moved in and we all gathered around my big square, wooden coffee table. Sally found a box of matches and lit one of my scented candles. Thankfully, it was a good one and smelled of a sea breeze rather than seaweed. Marisol was in the kitchen with Bardot, plotting something I'm sure I'll hate.

"What can I do, Halsey? Now that I have this big burden off my shoulders, I want to contribute."

"Thanks, Sally. We still have this story of the mechanics witnessing an argument with Jimmy and

Jonas. Did your cousin have any more insight on that?"

"None, except to say he would never pick a fight with anyone."

"Maybe I can help with that, I'm still employed by the *Times* and I'm doing a story on local general aviation, so I would have a valid reason to be asking questions."

"Brilliant, Mary Ann. I'll get the names of those guys from Jimmy and you can go to town."

"Thanks, Sally. I'm going to get right on this."

We watched her small frame shuffle to the door with purpose.

Sally sighed. "That still leaves me with a free hand, Halsey."

I looked at Peggy, and she took the floor.

"We've, well, Halsey has learned that this toxin that killed Jonas could also be extracted from a tree that grows here locally. It's called Angel's Trumpet. You may not recognize the name, but I'll guarantee you've seen the plant."

I pulled up an image on my cell and passed it around. There was instant recognition.

"Do you think you could check around here for examples?" I asked. "I'm specifically interested in knowing if any are growing near or around the Spitfire Grill, near the hangar where Rusty works, or the museum."

"Of course."

"Charlie and his buddies came through for us, and it turns out Chloe has a Nicaraguan boyfriend. Peggy's working that angle with the help of some of her past business associates.

"Damn right I am."

Marisol, I need you to go back to Rusty's mom to get more info on him. Also, find out if they have an Angel's Trumpet tree. Marisol?"

It was then that I realized she and Bardot were missing from the kitchen. I could hear double snoring coming from the hallway to my bedroom.

"Oh, she'd better not—"

We found Marisol passed out on my bed, sharing a pillow with Bardot.

CHAPTER 15

When I was able to wake Marisol with a loud foghorn noise from an app I'd downloaded, I filled her in on the mission she'd been assigned. I let her know we were now questioning Rusty's involvement, given that he wasn't flying the Pietenpol and kind of saved my life, but we still hoped his mom, Joan, might be the keeper of some clues. I gave her money to invite Joan to Spitfire Grill for turkey burgers. I said that if she could get the address for the apartment Jonas had been renting, I'd throw in another twenty-five bucks.

She squealed with delight.

I figured that would keep her occupied for a while and out of my hair. By now it was afternoon, so I checked the mail in perpetual hope that some of my invoices had been paid early. I needed something to wear to Malcolm and Penelope's wedding. Coincidently, their invitation was in my mailbox.

I ran my hand over the elegant, silver-embossed

script set onto an off-white linen heavy stock card. I had to admit weddings were fun, although I barely remember my own because I was so nervous. A sign I didn't heed. It should have been the most relaxed, peaceful, and fun day of my life. There had been so much that was right in the beginning; my ex was cool, creative, considerate and attentive. The guy knew how to court.

The Christmas after I'd turned thirteen, my dad got me one of those anthology book sets on Hollywood movies in the Golden Age. I immediately found the old movie stations on TV and spent that entire winter indoors, hooked on the sassy romances of Katharine Hepburn, Spencer Tracy, Cary Grant and Grace Kelly. I loved the female characters who were prim and proper on the outside but up for anything to get what they wanted in secret. And if they walked away at the end having taught someone an important lesson, all the better. So, like in the movies, I clung to the good parts of him, assuring myself I could change the parts that mildly bothered me and totally ignored the parts that were fundamentally opposed to my belief system.

Well, you live and learn.

I hopped online and typed "dresses for a Southern California afternoon wedding" into a search box.

Instead of the results being fancy dress shops and sites, the first link took me directly to lists of bridal shops. I decided to browse just for shiggles. I was alone in my office, so I began commenting aloud with each scroll to another picture.

"Not if it were the last dress on earth."

"Pretty, but I'd have to have my upper arms tucked first."

"No one has enough boob for that."

"Definite possibility, right, Bardot?"

She looked at me in a way that said, *not another oxymoron.*

"That style always looks like it was featured at a moth buffet first."

"Ack! It looks like something an albino threw up."

"Having fun?"

I nearly fell off my chair in shock when I saw Jack.

"I'm helping Penelope," I said, trying to quickly recover.

He just stood there grinning.

I punched a button on my keyboard and my screen went to black. To his credit, Jack didn't push it and moved on to the reason for his visit.

"I just came from the airport. I had to check in with Neil. We're doing a test rescue with the copter in the morning, and I wanted to make sure all the equipment was loaded. He was hanging outside shooting the breeze with another whirlybird pilot, and I asked him if he'd known Jonas."

"Good job. Had he?"

"Oh yes, and the things he told me may surprise you."

"You have my undivided attention."

Jack got a water for each of us out of the fridge and pulled a chair up next to me.

"First, he wasn't exactly the 'sweet boy,' as Britt described him, and she would know according to this fellow. It was known among the landing crews that Jonas had fallen hard for Britt and wasn't just pining away alone at night suffering from unrequited love."

"I'm both scared and excited to hear what you have to say next."

"I think you'll find it a bit of both. Neil's buddy and apparently a couple of others on separate occasions caught Jonas and Britt going at it hot and heavy in the flight simulator."

"Over what period of time? Had this been going on for over a year or more?'

"I asked the same question and that's the real sad part. All of this happened within the last month and a half. Which means Jonas was finally getting the girl of his dreams, only he didn't live long enough to enjoy it."

"Okay, my head is officially spinning, and you're nothing but a Jimmy-Stewart-in-*Vertigo* blur to me."

"I'm sorry, honey."

"Not your fault, and it was one of the scenarios we tossed around, the lovers' triangle between Britt, Rusty and Jonas. It assumed Rusty had a thing for Britt, which we haven't been able to prove yet. Crap, and I was just about to rule Rusty out."

Jack's phone came alive with a distinctive ring that told him this was a CARA emergency.

"Yes?"

Jack listened.

"How long ago? Okay, I think Neil is still at the airport. I'll get over there right away and we should be in the air in fifteen."

He dropped the call, then hit Speed Dial.

"Hey Neil, you still with the chopper? Great. Fire her up. I just got a call that an ultralight went down in Thousand Oaks."

Jack waved, blew me a kiss and ran out the door.

"Be careful!"

"Always."

I got into bed and decided to listen to a bit of music before going to sleep. Because of Marisol's proclivities for spying, I plugged in my headphones. I swear, I don't remember how I got there, but I found myself watching wedding videos on You-Tube. At first, they were the beautiful, love-filled videos that brought tears to my eyes—weddings in which I could picture myself and Jack as the bride and groom. But I soon slipped down the slope to the funny ones, like an outdoor ceremony where the best man trips on the dais while delivering the rings and knocks the bride and the minister into the pool behind them. Or the bride that chose five dachshunds as her bridesmaids and dressed them in pink gowns. And then there were the spectacular tumbles. Was I just working through jitters or was I truly not ready to do this again?

Just before my head hit the pillow and I passed out from exhaustion from the ordeals of the day, I got a text from Jack saying he was fine and they were still looking for signs of the downed plane. Knowing he was alive and well sent me down the rabbit hole and into a sleeping wonderland.

But not for long.

I dreamed that a giant black bear was on the

roof of my house and no amount of coaxing would lure him down. Everyone was urging me to call Animal Control so they could shoot him with a tranquilizer gun. I was afraid the bear would be severely injured in the fall, so I refused. If I teased my hair in all directions and became Freud for a minute, I would say the bear represented the big weight on my shoulders to solve this case, but because I didn't want the bear to be injured, I must be looking for the wrong killer.

What does Freud know?

When the sun was just about to make an appearance, I gave up on sleeping and decided to go for a swim. I'd had the foresight to throw the heat on in the pool yesterday because it was forecast to be a great, sunny summer weekend. Bardot ignored my movements and burrowed deeper into the bed.

I put on my Pamela Anderson red swimsuit and padded out the back. The air was still quite cool, so I grabbed two fresh towels and placed them near the pool steps. I would need to make a warm retreat to the shower when I'd finished my laps. I tightened my swim goggles and placed them on the top of my head. Long ago, I'd recognized the futility in wearing any sort of cap to keep my hair dry. They never worked. Even once in the dark of night, I'd tried an Esther Williams kind of full-head cover with a chin strap. It produced an angry red line across my forehead and neck.

The warm water felt divine on my feet, and just as I was about to do a swan dive, there was a loud splash that sent a wall of water my way. Bardot also must have realized bikini season was nigh.

I got into a rhythm doing laps, but that didn't convince Bardot that each turn was not a race. When I'd touch the wall at one end, she'd take off beside me and propel herself across the water with enough speed and ease to be able to look back and measure my slow-and-steady progress. She'd learned there wasn't much she could do to interrupt my routine for play, but that didn't stop her from swimming across the pool underwater to try to distract me. When I was one lap short of fifty, I stopped at one end. Bardot knew what that meant.

"Ready for the Olympic sprint?"

She lined up next to me and whimpered.

"Go!" I took off in a power kick, no-time-to-breathe swim. It was one back and forth in the pool for the gold. I didn't look up; I just kept my head down and worked every muscle in my body.

When my final stroke brought me to the wall, I let my whole being relax and slowly take in oxygen. I didn't see Bardot and yanked off my goggles in the hope that I'd finally beaten her.

"You owe me fifty dollars."

I looked to the side of the pool where the steps are and saw Marisol dangling her puce-painted toes into the water. Bardot was lying down next to her grinning—on the towels I'd placed there for when I got out.

It was going to be one of those days.

"Where did you come up with this fifty-dollar figure?" I asked Marisol after taking a long, warm shower and pulling on my coziest sweats.

She'd helped herself to the orange juice in my

fridge, which today was just orange juice, and she and Bardot were watching *The Today Show.*

"If you want to know what I know, show me the money."

I stared at her with snake eyes for a minute, trying to find out if she was bluffing. Ultimately, I went to get my purse.

"I presume this has to do with your lunch with Rusty's mom. What the hell did you guys order? It's nearly impossible to order over thirty dollars at Spitfire for a meal, let alone lunch."

"The money isn't for lunch."

"Marisol, what did you two do?"

"This has nothing to do with Joan, although she did tell me where Jonas lived, so thanks for reminding me. You owe me another twenty-five for that info."

"I'm going to owe you and deliver a knuckle sandwich if you don't start explaining yourself."

"Fine. You really aren't a morning person, are you?"

I turned off the TV and took her juice glass away from her.

"After lunch, I decided to check out the apartment building Jonas had lived in. It's just up a few streets on Centinela."

I stared back at her.

"The super was outside sweeping when I got there. Turns out, Larry and I went to Venice High together. From the looks of him, all he's been doing since then is eating his way through a Hostess factory."

She laughed. I didn't. "How do you live with

her?" Marisol asked Bardot. "Anyway, I told him that I was settling Jonas's estate, and that I needed access to his place."

"You did what?"

She nodded. "I may have said something about being an attorney too."

"You lied just to show off to a high-school alum? When he finds out and calls the cops, you'd better be ready to call in all your markers in the police department."

That didn't faze her a bit, but she grinned and pulled out a set of keys and dangled them in my face.

I moved to take them, and she quickly put them back in her pocket. Bardot sensed the beginnings of a game and sat up.

"What did you expect me to tell Larry? That I was with a mobile maid service and had been sent to mop the floors . . . sterilize the bathroom? Or that my crazy neighbor sent me on a spy mission to help clear her and her winos from a murder rap?"

"At least the second one would sound somewhat plausible coming out of your mouth."

"What's that supposed to mean?"

I took my wallet out of my purse, figuring she could go on like this all day and I'd end up actually killing her.

I pulled out the cash but gave her a taste of her own medicine and snatched it away when she reached for it.

"Tell me about these keys."

"Even your mother must hate you. Larry was happy to let Jonas's attorney into his apartment, but he said he was about to leave on a long week-end trip to Lake Elsinore and wouldn't be able to wait for me to finish and then lock up. So he gave me the keys and asked me to just drop them off on Monday. Or I could just take them off the ring and drop them into his locked mailbox slat."

With that, she dangled the keys again and held her other hand open with the palm up.

I counted out three tens and a twenty and placed the money in her hand. I reached for the keys, but she pulled them away again.

"Marisol, I'm calling Homeland Security right now and reporting your whole spying operation."

"You still owe me twenty-five for getting Jonas's address."

"I'm not paying it. This is extortion!"

"Have it your way." She tossed me the keys.

"You're giving up that easily? You must be spying on someone pretty interesting."

"Nope."

"So, what gives?"

"Those keys won't do anything but weigh down your pocket unless you know what building and door they open."

She laughed and laughed and laughed.

Later, I stared into my empty wallet and cried and cried and cried.

The apartment Jonas had rented was one of those late fifties/early sixties stucco boxes of about five stories facing busy Centinela Boulevard. Three-foot-deep small balconies gave the owners an excuse to charge a premium for the western-facing units, even though the only items that would fit out there were bicycles and folded-up card tables.

Because I was sure Marisol had already conducted a personal tour of Jonas's premises, I didn't even bother telling her that Sally, Peggy, and I were headed over there this afternoon. Heck, she probably knew anyway.

"You sure we won't run into the police, Halsey? We could do with a long time-out from Augie and the entire Pacific Police Department."

"Don't worry, Sally. Marisol told me she checked with the super, and the cops came by early on, swept Jonas's place, found nothing and moved on."

"Is this a wasted trip? We still have time to go back and rustle up a Wine Club," Peggy suggested.

"I think this is important. We agreed we need to learn as much about Jonas as possible. When the cops came by, all they were looking for were signs of a robbery or even signs of the murderer. We're going in to search for clues about his life and the people he considered important in it."

"You're right, of course, Halsey. I was just thinking about rainbow sherbet and Sauternes."

"Ew. Do you want tooth rot, Peggy? Tired of brushing?" Sally was leading the way along the fifth-floor hallway. "Sorry for that snipe, Peggy. The police are still sniffing around Jimmy, and it's left me in my cranky tights again."

"What's the number again, Sally?" We'd passed a door with a ragged mat piled with takeout menus.

"Five E."

"The E is missing, but we've checked all the other doors. Let's try the key," intrepid Peggy said.

It was dark on the floor, one of the fluorescent tube lights had burned out and it smelled vaguely of stale pot. Or a skunk. I doubt Jonas had ever brought the object of his desire, Britt, to this lair. I'd told Sally and Peggy the dirt on them while we were walking over. Like me, they found the news sad.

The key turned, and we entered the unit. Jonas had lived in a studio apartment in the back of the building overlooking an alley. From the little we'd been told about him, I think we all three expected to be entering a frat-house atmosphere, with a worn sunken couch, a big-screen TV, some artwork homage to beer and little else. That isn't what we found.

"Get a load of this." Sally held up a wooden carved sculpture of what looked like a giant anteater-type beast with a bushy tail.

"Creepy." I was trying not to focus on one item or another and just let the entire space tell me about the person who had lived in it.

"This is a person who traveled," Peggy noticed, doing pretty much the same thing I was. "No hometown California boy is interested in this kind of tapestry."

I followed her eyes and spotted the woven piece. It hung from a brass rod flush against the wall. It was made with brightly colored strips of several different wools and materials with a green fringe on the bottom, resembling long, hanging tree leaves. Beside it and on the same wall were three braided ropes with leather handles and a leather or shell pouch in the center. Sally came up beside me and examined the pieces.

"I know this sounds crazy, but I've been to my share of museums with Joe and this looks like pre-Columbian art."

"What do we think this kid was making at the airport as an apprentice to Rusty?" Peggy had joined us.

"Not enough to buy this kind of collection." I had no idea what to make of this.

"The origin of these items can't be a coincidence." I perused the titles on a two-shelf bookcase. There were lots of books on planes and flying from WWI to the present day. I noted some history books, all covering Central and South America. And at the very bottom, something caught my eye.

"This is going to knock you into the next century," I said to the girls after studying my find.

"Whatcha got there, honey?" Sally stopped nosing around the tiny kitchen and joined me back in the center of the room.

"It's a magazine. It was hidden behind a book on the bottom shelf. It's called *Pharmaceutical Processing*, and the corner of one of the pages is folded in."

"I hate when people do that." Peggy peered over my shoulder. "No, it can't be!"

Peggy snatched the periodical out of my hands for a closer look.

"*What?*" Sally asked, grabbing it from Peggy.

"That's right," I said. "Jonas or someone else bookmarked an article in the magazine authored by none other than our neighbor, Jeb Wallis."

"I need a drink," we all said at once and high-tailed it out of there.

We decided to forgo the elevator, which could be anywhere and take who-knows-how-long to arrive. This building just felt dirty with ugly secrets. As we were leaving, my cell rang, and I saw it was Jack.

"I've got good news and bad news," he said to me.

"Are you okay?" I felt a panic coming on.

"I'm fine. Where are you? I hear an echo."

"Long story, but I'm with Sally and Peggy. Should I put them on speaker?"

"Sure . . . hello, ladies. I'm heading back now. We got a report of an ultralight plane that went down in the hills near Thousand Oaks. We located the plane early this morning, but we found no sign of life or, for that matter, any indication anyone had suffered any injuries."

"How do you explain that?" Peggy asked.

"It's a tough one. I suppose the pilot could have parachuted out. But we haven't seen any remnants of that and we've flown over and over the area."

"I'm confused. Is this the good news or the bad news, honey?"

"Neither, Halsey. The good news is that the downed plane is a yellow Pietenpol Air Camper replica."

"Holy spicy Bloody Marys," Sally whispered.

"Wow. That sounds like the lead we've been waiting for. What's the bad part?"

"The bad part is that the tail numbers have been painted over and the plane is empty except for flying essentials. No paperwork, licenses, nothing to tell us who the owner is and who was flying it."

"That's not bad news," I said.

Everyone waited.

"That's the fat lady leaving the building. We're never going to solve this case."

CHAPTER 16

We were in a waiting game and I didn't like it. Everyone seemed to feel the same way, so we agreed to meet for lunch at Spitfire to pass the time. Maybe clues would just fall out of the sky and drop into our laps.

Jack had assured me that they were working on recovering the tail numbers, but I didn't hold out much hope. Whoever had downed that plane wanted everything to stay anonymous.

"Listen, you guys, I have something to tell you, but I can't do it here," Aimee whispered as we waited to be taken to our table.

"There are my girls!" Britt approached and went in for a group hug.

Somehow, I wasn't feeling it, but the others embraced her with aplomb.

"The usual booth?" she asked, grabbing menus.

Before they could all nod, I jumped in. "You know, it's such a beautiful day and I've been locked indoors working for the past week. How about we sit outside at the far end of the patio? Those who want sun can have it, and the others will be shaded by the umbrella."

"Okay," Britt said, giving me a good look.

"You are so brilliant," Aimee quietly told me as we marched back out the door of the restaurant.

We argued/discussed the seating arrangement, even though we were given a round table. There are nuances to the relationships within the Rose Avenue Wine Club I have never quite understood.

Ice teas and a hot coffee for Peggy were ordered and we got down to business. We had the patio pretty much to ourselves, except for a foursome of geeky guys who were engrossed in whatever version of their app they were beta testing. I felt confident we could speak freely. I studied the logo on the menu for a moment, trying to mentally compare it to the one on the business card in the gardening book. If they were different, it was subtle.

"I know we all have really interesting news to report, but let's try to go in an order that helps build the learning into a full story."

Mary Ann gave me an encouraging nod, probably sizing me up as possible editorial material.

"At the sister airport in San Diego," Peggy picked up the ball, "my sources tell me the Mexican restaurant hostess Chloe is quite the man magnet but has had a steady beau for almost a year now. This clown tosses around money like it grows on trees and is said to own a nightclub in Old Town. I'll have more on that in a day or so."

"How does that tie into our case?" Aimee asked.

"The guy's name is Oscar Sandoval and he comes from Nicaragua."

"The same country that was the source of the fish with the heroin." I could see light bulbs go off in everyone's mind.

"It's highly probable that drug runs have been happening from Montgomery for a while, courtesy of unsuspecting small plane pilots like Charlie. I'll smack that girl with a paddle if I see her again." Sally looked disgusted.

"Sorry. We just had a big rush inside," Britt said, returning to our table. "Let me get your orders in before the Mar Vista girls' soccer league beats you to the punch."

We did as she asked, and as Britt was rushing back, she stopped for a minute to admire a bulldog that one of the geeks had with him. A dim bulb was flickering in my brain as well. We spent the next few minutes slipping into our usual gossiping selves.

"My turn, I guess." Mary Ann sat up on the edge of her seat, anxious to give us the results of her work. We all leaned in so we could hear her soft voice. "I talked to the two guys who said they witnessed an argument between Jimmy and Jonas while they were working on a restoration in the open garage next to the museum hangar. They seem to be decent guys, and I have no reason to doubt they were sincere in their reporting."

She paused while our food was placed in front of us. I had the sinking feeling Mary Ann was about to divulge absolutely nothing in the way of help for Jimmy.

"Please go on, Mary Ann. Aimee, is that hot sauce in that caddy by you?"

"Here you go, Sally."

"I've been a reporter too long to just accept things at face value and not make sure I've looked at every side of the coin. I made them do a reenactment."

"I love this lady." Aimee hugged and nearly crushed her.

"You need to go on that sex show, the one where Chris Hansen catches those horndogs preying on young girls."

"I don't think so, Sally, but I appreciate the vote of confidence. As I suspected, things were not so clear when they took me through the paces. First off, the echo from that huge chamber distorts voices so much, it would be nearly impossible to understand what was being said from next door. Secondly, the only light in the hangar comes from those big overhead dome lamps or from sunlight seeping through a row of narrow, four-foot-long windows that run along one wall just under the roof. We shut off the lights and stood in the doorway from the garage and peered in. One of the mechanics stood in the place where they remembered Jonas was standing."

"This is so great, Mary Ann. I want to be you when I grow up." I said it and meant it.

"Agreed." Sally nodded while pouring more hot sauce on her vegetarian chili.

"Those windows are pretty old, and they refract any sun shining through. The effect is kind of eerie. There's an enlarged halo of light created when it hits the metal of the hangar wall and/or one of the planes stored in there."

"What you would see looking inside could be a Michael Jackson video, a close-up of twilight or the second coming?" Peggy had nailed it.

"Meaning this so-called argument and its participants would never hold up in court. Awesome work! I sent Marisol out on a recon mission and she had lunch with Rusty's mom. She wasn't able to get anything more to point guilt in his direction. He gambles, spends money he doesn't have and is generally disgusted with the world. But she said he has a good heart, and I can't argue, considering he saved me from a bad accident."

"Amen. Sorry that didn't pan out." Mary Ann said, draining her tea glass and looking around for someone to replenish it. For a five-foot woman, she sure had a couple of hollow legs.

"Never give up on Marisol. She came through big time," I corrected her and looked to Sally.

She recounted our search of Jonas's apartment and the unexpected artifacts and reading materials we found. She concluded by saying that there was still so much we didn't know about our murder victim.

I saw Aimee bouncing up and down on her chair like she was planted on a whoopee cushion and gave her the floor. Er, table.

Aimee took a long time to check all sides of us for eavesdroppers before she began.

"I bumped into Britt at the seafood stand in the Mar Vista Farmers' Market on Sunday. I know, kind of ironic that she was buying fish. But she also had a basket of produce she'd bought, so don't see too much into it. We decided to grab cappuccinos and take a load off at the food court. She wanted to know about Tom—how we met, you know . . . it was the perfect segue for me to turn the romance tables on her."

"You're a natural, honey." Sally toasted her with an empty tea glass.

"She told me about high-school crushes, a couple guys she'd been serious about and then stopped short of present day. I persisted and reminded her that she'd said that Jonas had had a thing for her. She seemed surprised I'd brought that up but then ultimately admitted—"

"You *chicas* all sated and happy?" Britt was back with the check and none of us had seen her coming. We'd all been so engrossed in Aimee's story.

"I think we're good," I replied, handing her my credit card. "Aimee's telling us some gory emergency room tales from Tom, and I don't think any of us could even look at food after what we've heard so far."

"Aimee, I'm shocked," she teased before walking away.

"You really should consider a post with the CIA, Halsey," Peggy whispered.

"Whew, that was close." Aimee fanned her increasingly crimson cheeks. "Okay, so she told me that she had a one-night stand with Rusty. He'd been at the bar all night, and she was in charge of closing up. One thing led to another. She said that now she's having trouble keeping him away, and she has no interest in him. I suggested she tell somebody in case he got aggressive, but she shook her head. She doesn't want to cause any trouble because she's new here. She told me she could take care of herself but didn't elaborate. Do you think she can? Do guys think we should do something?"

Sally, Peggy, and I shared a look.

"We're going to do something, Aimee, but not just yet. I promise you, though, the pieces to this puzzle are really falling into place."

As we walked to our cars, I noticed the geek's bulldog had been given a bowl of water.

When I returned home, I found Jack and Bardot playing in the pool. His giant schnauzer, Clarence, sat regally by the edge of the pool, but I could tell that as soon as Jack gave the nod, he'd be in as well. Jack could never take a break from training his dog.

"Hi honey, get on in. The water's great." He gave a short whistle, and Clarence pranced down the steps and into the water.

"Looks like you guys are having a blast." I laughed. "I'll be in soon. I've got some thinking to do. Jack, if I wanted to find out if someone had a pilot's license, how would I go about doing that?"

He thought about that for a bit.

"There are a bunch of private directories I have access to, but actually, the FAA database should have what you need, and it's public. You can do searches from the Airmen Inquiry section. Is there something I can help you with?"

"I just thought it might be a good idea to know who among our suspects has a valid pilot's license.

Maybe then we could do some kind of reverse lookup to trace one of them to the Pietenpol."

Jack swam over to the pool's edge, poised to get out.

"No honey, you relax and swim for a while in the warm water. You've been up for almost two days straight and you deserve a break."

He grinned like a kid who had been told he could finally go back in the pool after eating. Bardot was equally delighted to have her playmate back. I had one happy family.

In my office, I hopped onto my computer and navigated my way to the page I needed on the FAA's site. It displayed some basic search option fields, and the only one that was required was last name. I typed in Jack's info, just to test the system. Seconds later, it returned his credentials; address, medical information and a list and details of his certificates, including the dates they were issued.

Perfect, except for one little thing: I didn't know Britt's, Jonas's, Rusty's or Chloe's last names.

I next entered the name *Oscar Sandoval* and got three results, none of which looked like our Nicaraguan guy. No surprise there.

"Jack? What's Rusty's last name?" I shouted out to the pool.

"Mueller," he replied, his voice sounding nearby. I turned, and he was behind me, semidry, with a towel around his waist. Before I could say anything, he moved in for a warm, lingering kiss.

So cute, a girl could become distracted . . .

"Pull up a chair," I said, knowing where this was headed and wanting/not wanting to get back to my research. I typed in Rusty's last name.

"Nothing. Rats."

"Did you spell it with an *e*? As in 'M-u-e-l-l-e-r'?"

"Ah, that did the trick. And here's one from California. That must be him."

Jack scanned the data and nodded his head.

"How about Jonas's last name? Do you know his?"

"No clue. I don't suppose you want to ask Augie?"

"I'd rather have root canal while giving birth. I'm calling Sally."

She picked up right away but had to ask Jimmy.

"Peters," she said when she returned.

"What's the origin of that name?"

"German? Austrian? I can check."

"Thanks, Sally. What about Britt? Do we know hers?"

"No clue, but Aimee might. What's this all about?"

"I'm checking pilot's licenses for these guys, I thought it might help us tie up the last loose ends. I don't suppose you have Chloe's?"

"No way, but Peggy must have it, with her guys doing espionage for her."

"That's a strong word, Sally, but absolutely the right one. More later," I said and hung up.

A search for Jonas returned nothing, but Jack grabbed a laptop and consulted his secured directories.

Peggy didn't pick up, so I texted her. Same with Aimee.

"Now that's interesting," I heard Jack say after a couple of minutes.

"Interesting as in a lead? Because that's the kind of interesting we need."

"Then yes. I decided on a whim to check an international directory and I got a record for the name Jonas Peters."

"You sure that's the same Jonas? Remember, Rusty said Jonas was chomping at the bit to get his license, dying to get into the air."

"That was maybe for a domestic one."

"How can you be so sure this is our guy?" I peeked over Jack's massive shoulder.

"I'm not, but you keep telling me that I shouldn't believe in coincidences."

"You shouldn't. So?"

"So, this Jonas Peters has a license to fly in Nicaragua."

For that bit of good news, I took Jack's hand and pulled him outside, where I jumped up, wrapped my legs around his waist and gave him a big kiss. Bardot barked with glee, Jack gave me a questioning look and I nodded *okay*. I lowered myself down.

"On three," he said. "One—"

I couldn't wait and jumped in the pool, clothes and all.

CHAPTER 17

Believe it or not, sometimes bouncing thoughts off Marisol inspires me. I know that's about as hard to grasp as why you never see any baby pigeons, but all the same, I thought I'd give it a try.

Jack had gone home to crash, so I went around the block to our local convenience store and bought her a couple of ice-cold Yoo-hoos. Chocolate, of course, I refuse to indulge in her perverse craving for strawberry.

"Care for a nightcap?" I asked from the driveway side of her fence. I'd heard Marisol shuffling around back there, probably setting more finely tuned surveillance devices to point at my house.

"Haven't you had enough to drink today, Halsey?"

"It's not for me, it's for you. Or should I say Yoo-hoo?"

"You can come in, I guess."

I reached over the top of the gate and undid the

latch. She was already dressed for bed in a long nightgown, fuzzy pink robe and thick Christmas-themed socks. She was taking dried laundry off the line that ran horizontally across her yard. Marisol owns a dryer, but as she says, *As long as there's sun in the sky, I'm not using any damn machine.* I pointed out that there are also rivers and rocks, but she seemed to think the same didn't apply to her washing machine.

Marisol is somewhere between eighty-seven and one hundred and seven, but you wouldn't know it to look at her. She scampers around wherever she needs to go, she is always learning new things, some devious, and is devoted to her family. I noticed she was taking in some of her daughter Terry's exercise clothes, even though she is perfectly capable of doing her own laundry at the age of forty-two.

She grabbed both drinks out of my hand, and we sat down on two patio chairs. They were the metal kind from the fifties that bounce if you swing yourself back and forth on their tube base, but these weren't some retro knockoffs. These were the real thing.

Of course, she had to bounce as she drank.

"Marisol, I wanted to pick your brain on this whole airport mess and murder."

"What's the matter with your brain? Is it embalmed already?"

"Very funny. You have a way sometimes of seeing things from your own twisted view, which is just what I think this case needs."

"Of course it is. What do you want to know?"

This was no time to pull punches, so I told

Marisol everything I knew, including Jonas and Britt's sordid affair.

"So sweet, young Jonas is a big, fat liar. A lot of guys are, especially if they're trying to get into a girl's pantaloons."

"But wouldn't showing he actually has a pilot's license be more impressive?"

"He must have wanted to keep a low profile, to hide what he was really doing at the airport."

"Which is what, Marisol?

"The stuff in that kid's apartment didn't look like it came from a dumpster dive. That had to cost money. Sure, the building was crap; that's what he wanted people to see. I asked the super and he said Jonas never had visitors."

"You think he was secretly making beaucoup bucks from the drug deals?"

"Well, it wasn't Rusty. His mama told me again that she had to loan him money. Same old story. The people at the bottom do all the work while the bosses get the rewards."

I thought about that for a moment.

"Do you think Rusty was actually working for Jonas?"

"Glad to see your brain isn't entirely shot."

"That would mean Jonas was the one with ties to the San Diego airport."

I got my phone out to call Peggy, but before I could dial, I got a text from her.

Hi. Chloe's last name is Bird. I know, it sounds cuckoo!

"You ever hear of a person named Chloe Bird?" I asked Marisol.

"Sounds like a stripper's name, and those days are long gone for me."

For a moment, I just stared at her, and she grinned back.

"She works at that restaurant in San Diego and her boyfriend is probably smuggling drugs from there to the Santa Monica airport. If you're right about Jonas, I now have to link him to this Chloe Bird."

"Of course I'm right. You got another Yoo-hoo? If not, I'm going to bed."

Like clockwork, as I was blearily sipping my morning tea, I saw Sally barreling up Rose Avenue on her morning workout. She'll complete five thousand steps before I've even brushed my teeth. From the window in my breakfast nook, I saw her stop in front of my house.

I opened the window and stuck my head out.

"You can't be tired already."

"I'm not. I was trying to decide if you were up."

"I'm up. Come in and I'll fix you a nice cup of tea. You can jog in place if you need to keep up with your step count."

"Ah," Sally said, sipping her glorious brewed elixir. "How nice, and I don't even mind cutting my exercise short. This is the only time of the day I have to myself."

"Really? How come?"

"The boys are on their own for breakfast, which generally means they eat cereal. God forbid they should attempt to put a slice of bread into the toaster. Then, if Joe is home, he gets his allergy shot around noon. He really is suffering right now. I don't know if it's because of the time of year or if he's just so agitated by the police hanging around outside and watching the house. Joe's new favorite activity is turning on the sprinklers when the cops step out of their car to stretch their legs."

"That's a total Marisol move." I laughed. "Then I suppose you start thinking about dinner. Isn't Jimmy borderline diabetic?"

"Yes, and so I have him on a special diet. What he does when he's working at the museum is his choice, but when I feed him, he's going to eat right."

"Amen, sister!" I thought for a moment. "That's a lot of responsibility on your shoulders, Sally, even when you aren't facing possible prison time for yourself or your family. You do it so effortlessly, I don't think I realized how much pressure you have to deal with. I'm going to make it my personal mission to whisk you away on fun adventures as often as you'll let me."

"I love it! And no time like the present. Get dressed; we're going shopping!"

"Guess who has a pilot's license?" I asked Sally as she drove.

We were headed to IKEA, where she needed to pick up new armchair covers and "while I'm at it," she told me, more wineglasses. It sounded like a fine way to spend a morning, and I could already taste the meatballs with lingonberry sauce I planned to devour for lunch.

"Marisol?"

"Ha! She might, but I meant Jonas."

"A student license; we knew that."

"No, Sally, a full-on, legit license."

She looked at me with raised eyebrows and I brought her up to speed.

"Wow, that's making my head spin."

"Don't do that while you're driving." I chuckled. "But it gets more interesting. His license is international and was issued in Nicaragua."

"Is there smoke coming out of my ears, 'cause my brain's on fire!"

That elicited a full laugh from me. It was so nice to see Sally back to her silly, sarcastic, jolly self.

"Guess who else?" I wasn't done blowing her mind.

"I give up."

"Chloe Bird."

"Who the sand dabs from Chez Jay's is Chloe Bird?"

"Our waitress from Casa Machado in San Diego."

"That's her name? I wouldn't have remembered, I was so upset at the time with Jimmy's fate. So? That doesn't seem like a big deal. She works at an airport, after all."

"It isn't, except for the fact that it makes her another suspect who can fly."

"How many do we have now?"

"Rusty, Jonas, presumably Oscar Sandoval and his girlfriend, Chloe Bird."

"And you think they're all connected?"

"It's looking more and more that way."

"Are we missing anyone else?"

"Just Britt, I asked Aimee if she could get her last name."

We pulled into the parking lot of the huge blue and yellow emporium of all things modern and reasonably priced. I remembered my first trip to an IKEA years ago, and the feeling I might never find my way out. It wasn't such a bad thing because I felt like I was in a kind of Disneyland for first-time homeowners and singles finally able to ditch the beanbag chairs. Sally apparently knew her way around this store. She dragged me to the escalators, and when we reached the top entrance, she dragged me again.

"Come with me. I know a way to cut through all these room settings and get to where we want to go."

"You mean the cafeteria?"

"Not quite yet, silly. We need to stop at the stemware, fabrics, doodads and thingamajigs section first."

"Fine by me. I haven't had a good Swedish doodad in a while."

"Halsey! There are children here."

"What? It's true."

We cut through a denim blue-and-white living room, and it was everything I could do to keep up with Sally. That sofa and chaise with all the soft pillows was calling my name, and I wondered if the cafeteria delivered.

Sally brought us to an elevator in the back corner and we waited to board the oversize cage that could accommodate at least two shopping carts as well as people. Just as the doors opened, my cell phone rang. My current ringtone is that of a breathy woman's voice saying, *If it's not one thing it's another*—over and over. People laughed at first and then less, so I quickly answered.

"Hi Aimee! Sally and I are at IKEA picking up a few things."

"Oh, wow, I was just there. Can you be a dear and get me two more packages of the dish towels I love so much? They fit in great at the Chill Out."

"Sure. Do they have a name?"

"Lemme look; I'll be right back. Yes, they're called, geez, I'll never be able to pronounce this. I'll spell it for you. S-o—"

"Hang on. I need a pen."

At that, three people on the elevator offered me an IKEA pencil. When I looked around again, I was handed an order slip to write on.

"Okay, go."

"S-o-m-m-a-r-g-l-i-m. They're real cute. You should get some for yourself."

"I just might. Is that why you called?"

"How would I have known you were at IKEA? No, that's not why I called, but I'm glad I did. I got your text and Britt's last name is Fagel. F-a-g-e-l."

I wrote that down on the same slip.

"Great. Thanks, Aimee. I'll bring your towels over as soon as we get back."

I gave a nod of gratitude to all my administrative assistants.

"That's a funny name," Sally said, glancing at the slip after we disembarked on a lower floor.

"You want funny? They have a wardrobe named *Dombås*."

"No, I meant Britt's last name—not one you hear every day."

We separated for a bit to browse the floor. I was dying to put the name Britt Fagel into the FAA's database, but it would have to wait until I got home to my computer. I would have preferred to go back upstairs to one of the bedroom settings and think all this through—maybe grab the *Måla* easel and paper on the way to take notes. But I knew that wouldn't fly, so I just ambled around the kids' toy area. My phone rang again and this time it was Peggy.

"Hi!"

I decided not to let on that we were at IKEA; I could only imagine what she would have wanted us to get for her, and I was now anxious to get back to Rose Avenue.

"Hi back, Halsey. I've got some news for you, such as it is."

"Uh-oh. That doesn't sound very promising."

"Remember what I told you, every bit of information has the capability of blowing this thing wide open when looked at it from all angles?"

"Right."

"I talked to the guys who've been looking into our friend Oscar Sandoval in San Diego. They came up empty. No driver's license, no bank accounts, no visas. In fact, there's no record of him ever entering the country."

"How is that possible? He owns a nightclub. He had to have leased the space and he's got to pay utilities. I guess he could pay his employees in cash."

I was sitting on a children's plastic blue stool at a matching mini dining table. I'd pushed the colorful plastic place settings and cups to one end so I could take notes on my order slip.

"It's possible because none of that is in Oscar's name. It's all paid for by a conglomerate out of Vegas calling themselves Beeskow Enterprises. What's that noise? Where are you?"

I looked up and noticed a group of kids had decided that the toys around where I was sitting were the best they'd ever seen, and they'd gone into playacting a *Top Chef* challenge. I got up and moved to the shopper's path, which was lined with wire baskets brimming with little things to amuse the kiddies, like finger puppets, plush animals and wooden cars and trains.

"Sorry about that, Peggy, I was fiddling with the car radio, trying to find a weather report."

Who am I to try to lie to Peggy? I'm stopping off in purgatory for sure now.

"Oh-kay. So, of course we're working on getting details about this enterprise, but because it's registered out of Vegas, it's probably a shell company. When we're done with the research, we'll probably find it's being run by a fellow by the name of Dirk Diggler."

Peggy's a Boogie Nights *fan? Oh my!*

"Thanks, Peggy. I've got one more name I need you to check out," I said, distracted by something

I'd spotted in one of the bins. As I walked over to it, I told Peggy what I needed.

"There you are. I got everything I wanted." Sally pulled up with an overflowing shopping cart. "What are you staring at?"

"Sally, we've got to get home right away!"

CHAPTER 18

I agreed to wait for Sally to check out and went outside and waited by the car.

"Jack?"

"Hi honey. I was just thinking about you."

"You have anything more on the Pietenpol?'

"Oh, all business for Halsey today. Nothing yet on the ownership, but the DEA's been all over it, checking for drug residue. I can give my friend, Agent Mark, a quick call to see what he and his team have found."

"They'll find heroin: traces of it, at least."

"You sound like you know something I don't."

"Actually, a few things. And we're going to need to talk to Mark. Do you think you can get him to meet us somewhere tonight?"

"I'll check. Do I get to tell him what this is about?"

I gave him the top line and what I thought we

should do about it. I could see Sally coming out of IKEA and told Jack I had another call to make.

"Hey Peggy."

"Twice within the hour. You must really love me."

"I do, and I need you. Any chance you could convince Charlie to fly into Santa Monica airport in the next day or two?"

"I don't know why not. If I tell him I'm making my pot roast, he'll probably hang glide here with a good tailwind."

"I don't want him doing that. He's going to have cargo with him."

Sally had opened the trunk, and I motioned for her to come over and listen in. She did as I explained the plan.

"See?" Sally said as we merged onto the freeway. "IKEA really does have everything."

Jack and I met Mark at Chez Jay's in Santa Monica. A beloved landmark, this nautically themed watering hole on Ocean Avenue first opened its porthole in 1959. The Jay in Chez Jay's is Jay Fiondella. As the story goes, he was a two-bit actor, hustler and bartender on the Santa Monica pier when he spotted a "For Sale" sign on a coffee shop across the street from the pier. He scraped together enough to buy it and turned it into a favorite steak-and-seafood dive that attracted the famous to the trademark-free peanuts and sawdust floor. It has flourished ever since. Mark was sitting at the bar, nursing a tap beer.

"Hey buddy," Jack said, shaking his hand and offering me the stool next to Mark's.

"Hi Jack, Halsey. Good to see you."

Mark and Jack had met through dogs, of course. Mark was training to become a K-9 team with the DEA, and Jack had been brought in to consult. The two hit it off and have remained friends. Mark works undercover, which suits him just fine because I've never seen him in anything else but jeans and a Hawaiian shirt. Maybe a Members Only Windbreaker if it's raining. I once asked Jack if those were his regular clothes or just for work and he shrugged. Mark was around Jack's age, I guessed, and I'd seen him in action, and he could be extremely athletic and fierce when he was about to make an arrest.

Jack signaled for two more beers for us and secured a supply of shelled peanuts. He stood behind my barstool, and when we leaned in to talk, we had a fair amount of privacy. Plus no one in here was interested.

"I understand you're making my job easy again, Halsey."

"I'm not sure about that, but I did get access to some information that may help."

"I'm anxious to hear it."

"Me too, hon." Jack patted my back.

"Okay, I'll start at the beginning just to make sure I tell you everything I know. Our friend, Charlie, flew in from San Diego's Montgomery Airport several weeks ago and hit something on the runway, which caused him to crash. I still don't know what that was. The accident brought in the cops, who discovered that a cooler Charlie had been asked to transport was loaded with fish stuffed with heroin. The fish could have come from only one place: Lake Managua in Nicaragua."

"Yep, my team was called in to investigate that afternoon. I hadn't heard about the fish origin, though."

"Mark told me there has been some bad stuff circulating that's cut with fentanyl. They've been working this for a while."

Mark nodded.

"Then—and we've been debating whether this is connected to the drug smuggling or not—Jonas, a kid we were told was apprenticing for the landing-crew chief, Rusty, was found killed with something very lethal."

"Devil's Breath; I know you've had dealings with it, Mark," Jack picked up the story.

"Boy, have I, though never stateside. Mostly, I'd get involved when American tourists visiting Colombia were involved. And I've only ever encountered one death from it."

"Apparently, this was some heavy, powerful dose, according to the autopsy report. Should we order some steamed clams and maybe a crab cocktail? I'm starving," Jack announced.

"Sounds good, and I'd like a glass of Chalk Hill Chardonnay," I said, sliding the remainder of my beer over to Jack.

Life is too short to drink beer when you can have wine.

"The Rose Avenue Wine Club then set to work

to try to solve this crime. We had a vested interest because one of our members was accused of buying unregulated prescription drugs and her cousin was being looked at for Jonas's murder."

My wine arrived, and I took a fortifying sip.

"Where does this Pietenpol replica I've been testing fit into the equation?"

Jack told Mark about the flyover and the sightings, both here and in San Diego.

"It ties in because we found plans to build that exact plane tucked away in the hangar where Rusty has his desk."

"Ah, but without tail numbers and no filed flight plans, we can't make a more solid connection?"

"Unfortunately, Mark, but I have a theory about that."

"I'll bet you do." He laughed.

Our food arrived, and we spent a few minutes savoring our fresh, sweet seafood.

"I can see already that we're going to need another order of clams, and how's a shrimp quesadilla sound?" Jack said to the bartender and looked at us.

All we could do was nod. We were too busy eating.

"We made a trip to Montgomery Airport and had lunch at the Mexican restaurant that sits off the runway. Charlie had remembered that the guy who brought the fish cooler to his plane was wearing a shirt with a Casa Machado logo on it; that's the name of the restaurant. We met the hostess/

waitress, a girl named Chloe. She was friendly at first, but when we started asking questions about the fish, she shut down and sealed up tighter than a sous vide salmon. We later learned she has a boyfriend named Oscar Sandoval, a flashy guy from Nicaragua who runs a nightclub in San Diego."

"You've established a connection to this guy Oscar and the smuggled heroin found at Santa Monica airport. Give me a minute. I want to get someone working on finding Sandoval and collecting evidence. What's the name of the nightclub?"

Jack and I exchanged looks.

"Er, Mark, let's just say for now that people are already on Oscar Sandoval's case. Don't worry, it's all legit, and I feel safer knowing he's being handled. We have something more urgent we need to bring you in on."

Mark was taken aback and gave me a long, hard look. He was about to say something when Jack piped up.

"I'll explain it to you later. One of our US agencies is on the case."

Mark looked like he wanted to press it, so I quickly continued.

"We then turned our efforts to learning more about the victim, Jonas. We thought if we knew what he was up to, it might tell us why someone would want him dead. We got access to Jonas's apartment—"

Mark was about to, no doubt, ask if we broke in, but Jack again waved him off.

"What we found were valuable artifacts, tapestries and books that resemble pre-Columbian art. Certainly something a kid working for peanuts to get his pilot's license couldn't afford."

"We also found out," Jack said, pulling away a wedge of quesadilla, "that he was already an internationally licensed pilot. He was certified in Nicaragua."

I thought Mark was going to choke on a clam.

"There was apparently some sort of love triangle going on between Jonas, Britt—she's a waitress at Spitfire Grill—and Rusty. Both guys were hounding her. It seems Jonas had more success, if you believe the rumors."

"You think that maybe Jonas was running this drug ring using Oscar and maybe Chloe in San Diego and Rusty up here?"

"Yes," Jack said.

"Wow. That is some investigating you and the ladies of the Rose Avenue Wine Club have done. Ever consider working undercover?"

Jack laughed. I thought about it, which made him squirm a bit.

"There's one last bit that ties this all together and is why we need to set up a sting," I said, finishing the last of the crab cocktail and motioning to the bartender for another glass of wine.

"A sting? Now you're getting way ahead of yourself. We can't rush into anything or we could tip them off and end up with nothing."

Mark was looking nervous. He'd heard from Jack how hard I am to rein in.

"Chloe's last name is Bird."

"So? Could easily be a fake."

"True, Mark. Britt's last name is Fagel."

This time he just stared at me.

"Fagel is the Swedish word for bird. Chloe and Britt are sisters."

CHAPTER 19

Of course we were told to stay as far away from the airport as possible.

Of course we didn't.

It had taken a few more days to set everything in motion, and while that was going on, we managed to fit in a Wine Club, courtesy of Aimee. We elected not to invite Britt.

Aimee outdid herself, as she always does. If she doesn't open a full restaurant soon, we may all have to sit on her until she does. Today, she'd adopted a German/Swedish theme, which we would all later find very apropos. She had made ham and cheese croquettes, homemade pretzels with a spicy mustard dipping sauce, meatballs and pineapple skewers and some sort of German beer cheese spread that you were supposed to eat with apple slices. Most of us quickly discovered that dipping the meatballs in it made for a delicious combination.

Hearing the menu, I'd brought along a flight of rosés. We were heading into summer, and a world tour of wines I'd been meaning to try seemed like just the thing. Rosé haters, I double dog dare you to feel the same way after sampling these. Here's what I brought:

Paraduxx Napa Valley Rosé
Pittnauer Rosé, Austria
Rideau Vineyard Rose, Santa Ynez
Mulderbosch Cabernet Sauvignon Rosé,
    South Africa

"I want to thank you all for coming, I know we've all been busy gathering information on this horrible tragedy that took place at the airport. I can't wait until it's resolved and we can get back to our normal lives." Aimee was tearing up already.

"I'm starting to think this *is* our normal life, thanks to the curse."

We'd all forgotten about that little wrinkle until Sally brought it up again.

"You really don't think that's anything more than a Rose Avenue myth, do you, Sally?"

"I do, Mary Ann, and I don't think it ever really went away. I think it's been festering underground all these years and the crash brought it back."

That reminded me that I still hadn't figured out what had caused said crash. This was really frustrating me.

"Everyone have a full glass of wine?" Peggy asked. She had her iPad with her, which meant new news was on the way.

We all settled down and looked to her.

"I have answers to a few loose ends that can now be tied up. Jonas, last name Peters, although now a US citizen, was born in Germany. When he was very young, the family moved first to Colombia and later to Nicaragua. There's a large expat community in each country," Peggy consulted her tablet, "mostly moving there after WWII, when agricultural and technical experts were sorely needed and solicited. In the case of the Peters, they needed to leave town before the father was arrested for a long list of petty crimes."

"I can see where this is going."

Peggy held up her iPad. On the screen was a photo of a rather handsome dark-haired man with very light skin. He looked like a Teutonic version of Daniel Day Lewis, with a little Sam Shepard thrown in for good measure. I could see the likeness in Jonas.

"Is the father still alive?"

"As far as my people know. Why do you ask, Halsey?"

"Because Augie told us early on that they busted the owners of a nightclub in Colombia for selling Devil's Breath to their patrons. Maybe the dad was part of this and that's why they fled to Nicaragua. Can you check to see if his name is associated with any club business there? And you might as well attach the name Beeskow Enterprises to the search. That's the company that owns Oscar's club in San Diego."

"That's using the old bean, Halsey."

Impressing Peggy always gave me a thrill.

"It seems our girl Britt is knee deep in this mire too. In addition to being Chloe's sister, Halsey checked, and she does have a pilot's license." Sally said this while trying to "unpretzel" a pretzel.

"Aw, geez, and here I thought she was so nice, we were becoming friends. We had plans to go out to dinner, a foursome. Tom was bringing a guy from work."

"I wouldn't do that if I were you. We know Britt and Jonas were caught in flagrante delicto in the flight simulator and look what happened to him."

"Wait, what now, Halsey?" Sally looked bewildered.

"They were doing the nasty courtesy of NASA," Peggy explained.

"Were they in zero gravity? That could prove difficult."

"What do you know about the sting, Halsey?" Mary Ann asked, thankfully changing the subject.

"Right. Tomorrow, Charlie is going to fly up here from San Diego. In his plane will be a cooler, only this time it will only be filled with ice. Just before landing, he's going to call Rusty to let him know he has some cargo he'll be dropping off."

"The DEA will be waiting and ready to arrest everyone anxiously awaiting the delivery. The idea is to get them to talk, and then make the necessary arrests in San Diego as well."

"Peggy, is this at all risky for Charlie?" Aimee grabbed a couple of croquettes. She eats when she's nervous.

"Shouldn't be. There will be agents all around."

"What about us? Do we just wait patiently at home for the news?"

"Have you met us, Mary Ann? Let's all take a knee and huddle," I said.

The scene of the bust was once again going to take place in front of Rusty's hangar. Jack had come just shy of locking me in the bathroom when he left to meet Mark, but I'd assured him I had no intention of leaving the house. I'd left out the *before noon* part. I'd now lied to both Peggy and Jack, and I was starting to think that on Judgment Day there would be only one direction I'd be headed.

I decided not to waste my time arguing with Marisol about coming along. She'd only follow us anyway and she'd been a big help in this case. I put her in charge of Bardot, to make sure she'd be safe, and then wondered if Bardot would be safe with her.

We decided to retrace the route we'd taken before, when we searched Rusty's place, but in the light of day we had to take extra precautions not to get caught. The entire Wine Club was in attendance. It was Aimee who'd had the brilliant idea for our cover. She said it came to her when she was stuck in traffic on the 405 for an hour the day before.

We gathered at the east end of the airport disguised in caps, sunglasses and orange vests while carrying yellow trash picker sticks. We'd decided that rather than trying to sneak to the hangar, we'd work our way around to it in plain sight, picking up trash along the way. This wasn't easy, considering the temperature had already risen to ninety.

"Ew, is that a dead possum?" Aimee asked.

"Those can be good eatin' if you marinate them properly and cook 'em long enough." Sally took a look at Aimee's quarry.

"That's okay. I just became a vegetarian."

We had to time our arrival just right or we could miss the whole bust. I'd asked Charlie to text me when he was five minutes out. We were making progress, and whenever a golf cart came by with someone in authority driving, we all pretended to be picking strawberries with our heads down and backs hunched. No one seemed to notice or care. I looked back to make sure we were all keeping together and saw that Bardot was straining on the end of the leash Marisol was holding. Bardot must smell a particularly inviting critter. As I headed over to relieve Marisol, I saw her reach down and undo the leash's clasp.

"No!" But I was too late, and Bardot was racing through the tall grass in the direction of the hangars.

"What? You try holding back a locomotive," Marisol spat.

That was when I noticed that instead of a trash picker, we must have been one short. She was holding a piece of vacuum cleaner wand with the crevice tool attached on the end. It doubled as a walking stick.

"It's okay," I said, feeling in a generous mood, "I'll give Bardot a long bath and tooth brushing to clean away all the critter juice tonight."

"Can I come?"

I felt my phone vibrate and checked it. There was a text from Charlie:

Oops, forgot!

I looked up to see a plane making its approach. "Come on, we've got to hurry!"

We knee-high stepped it over the field and made our way to the back door of Rusty's hangar. Bardot was nowhere in sight.

Once inside, we quietly crept forward along a side wall. I could see Rusty standing at the mouth of the hangar facing the runway. I turned around and put my index finger up to my lips, indicating to the girls that we must be quiet. Thankfully, the sound of Charlie's engines helped mute any sounds we made.

We watched as Charlie circled his plane back around upon landing and pulled up in front of Rusty. Charlie left it idling and hopped out.

"How you doing, Rusty? Hot enough for you? When I left San Diego, it was already pushing triple digits."

"Hey. You have any idea who this cargo is for? I wasn't aware of anything coming in today."

"Nope. Some kid from Casa Machado drove it up to my plane and stowed it. Just like always."

"What do you mean 'like always'? You're not our regular trans—"

Rusty caught himself, but it was too late.

"*Freeze.* Put your hands up where I can see them." I saw Mark come out from around the outside of the hangar. He was pointing a gun and was

flanked by two other DEA men. There was no si
of Jack.

Rusty complied. "You don't understand. I v
just the middleman. I really didn't want any part
this; forget the money, it wasn't worth it. I was t
ing to get out."

Rusty's long blond hair had fallen into his fac
making him look like a scared little boy. Ma
moved in and cuffed him.

"If what you say is true, who was running t
show, Rusty?"

Mark watched as his men frisked him for a
concealed weapons.

"Jonas, that's who. The kid had been runni
drugs since his teens out of Nicaragua. He broug
in the girls, and they were pretty good at manip
lating people to do what they want. Even co
vinced me to loan them my plane."

"The Pietenpol?" Jack appeared from arou
the side.

Rusty nodded. "Not my plane, really. Jonas loan
me the money. I was paying him back by helpi
unload the drug cargo and get it to the local de
ers. Britt likes to fly it real low and scare people.

"That's a load of crap," Britt said, arriving on
golf cart with a tray of food from Spitfire. "Y
can't believe a word that comes out of this gu
mouth. He's a lowlife petty crook and he's be
harassing me for sex since I started working
Spitfire. Ask anyone."

"Now I know why Chloe looked so familia
Charlie said. "I've seen you two together in th
very hangar."

"Keep out of it, old man." Britt dropped the tray and pulled a gun on Charlie.

I heard Peggy gasp.

"Who's back there? You'd better come out. You've got five seconds before your pilot friend is grounded for good."

To back this up, Britt grabbed Charlie by the arm and pointed the gun at his head. I motioned for everyone to go out while I stayed behind. Hopefully, Britt wouldn't be doing a head count.

"You need to put the gun down, miss. There are too many people here to stop you. Before you pull the trigger, we'll be all over you. Now, surrender before you get hurt." Mark was even scaring me, and we were on the same side.

"Ha!" Britt laughed when she saw the Wine Club girls emerge. "It was you bitches. You ruined everything with your nosiness. Why couldn't you just stick to your platters of radishes and rosés?"

"Britt, I thought we were friends. We still could be if you give up now."

Wow. Aimee gets the Medal of Honor for bravery.

I saw a shadow moving along the other wall of the hangar. It was a person, but I couldn't tell who. I looked to Mark, trying to get his attention without revealing myself. So far, I was the only one who could call for help. I saw him make eye contact with Jack, and I suspected they were developing a nonverbal plan.

"Where's Oscar Sandoval, Britt?" Jack inched a bit closer to her.

"Long gone, I'm guessing. Once he downed the

plane, he'd planned to disappear for a couple of months. Not that he was ever here."

"And your sister? Where's she?"

"Well, aren't you all so clever, figuring that out? Chloe's in San Diego as far as I know."

I bet not.

Just then, we heard the engines of Charlie's plane start back up, and I saw the passenger side door swing open. Through the center of the hangar, I saw a low, dark figure race by.

"Bardot!"

I raced after her, and out of the corner of my eye, saw Britt become distracted. Jack moved in quickly and disarmed her.

Bardot leaped airborne and landed in the plane's passenger seat. I turned on my jets and ran and did the same. In the pilot's seat, just as I thought, was Chloe. I tried wrestling her for the controls but couldn't get much of a grip as I was draped facedown over the passenger seat. She was trying to push me out, but Bardot kept fighting her off.

"Fine. I'll dump you both over the ocean. It'll be tidier that way."

I felt the plane move and heard Mark get on his radio.

"Halsey!" Jack's shout was sounding farther away as we kept rolling.

The door to the cargo hold was still open, and I could see him get smaller and smaller as the plane gathered speed. I could also hear sirens coming from the tarmac. I held on tight to Bardot and asked the Big Man for absolution for lying to

Peggy and Jack. Then Chloe made a sudden acceleration to lift off the tarmac, sending a whiplash through the cabin. I saw the cooler sail out the back and crack open on the runway.

If this is the last thing I see, at least I've solved a riddle.

CHAPTER 20

Moments later, I heard tires screeching as Chloe applied the brakes. The airport trucks had arrived in time to thwart her takeoff, and other than a head and neck ache, I was okay. Bardot was fine too. She'd picked up Chloe's scent, remembering it from the rag she'd placed under her water dish at Casa Machado. Bardot must have concluded that Chloe needed to be found and took off hunting for her. This taught me once again that Bardot's brain was a powerful sponge for knowledge.

Cue the music: "The more you knowwwww."

When everything and everyone was secured or taken into custody, I walked over to the broken cooler sitting on the runway. Just as I'd thought, the ice that had spilled out had melted and dissipated on the tar and in the heat. Which I knew now was exactly what had happened after Charlie hit a pile of ice on the day of the crash. It had been a similar hot day, and when Jonas started work that morning, he must have unpacked the drug shipment that had come in the night before. I'm guessing he tossed the ice out of the hangar and onto the runway.

"Charlie's going to be so happy to hear about this," Peggy said, coming up next to me and surveying the damaged cooler.

Jack and Mark walked toward us with the rest of the girls.

"Let's go back to the administrative office for a debriefing. We'll be away from the noise and it's air-conditioned." Mark led the way.

I was trying desperately to avoid eye contact with Jack. I could tell he was really pissed at me. I ran to catch up with Sally and Aimee.

"You may run now, Halsey, but we're going to talk about this," I heard him holler at me.

You know me well enough now to guess how that sat with me.

We gathered in their conference room, and a kind officer brought in a case of waters for us. I shared with Bardot.

"Here's the problem," Mark began.

"There's a problem? How can there be a problem? Didn't you just arrest three people for drug dealing out there?" I heard my voice go up at the end and tried to calm myself. That went right out the window when I saw Augie enter the room.

"Hey Augie, thanks for joining us. You're correct, Halsey. The DEA is going to prosecute Rusty, Britt and Chloe to the full extent of the law. But that's for drug dealing. If we catch this Oscar Sandoval, the same goes for him. But they all deny knowing or having anything to do with Jonas's murder and it's hard to argue with that. Why bite the hand that's feeding them so well?"

"Aw dingleberries, we'd better not be back to Jimmy again," Sally said.

"No, it's more like we're back to zero," Augie spoke up.

"But—" I realized I had no argument. I looked around the room but got no backup. The girls were all starting to leave. Mary Ann really seemed to take it badly.

"You coming, Marisol?"

"Nah, Halsey. I got a flying lesson."

Peggy suggested a Wine Club, but no one was in the mood. We walked to Rose Avenue dragging our orange vests behind us.

"We're back to the age-old question," I said.

"Chicken or egg?"

"No, Sally. Is Jonas's murder connected to the drugs or not?"

As we rounded the corner and headed down the hill, I saw Jack's truck parked outside my house. Call me a coward, but I wasn't in the mood for a fight, and this would be a big one. No man is ever going to control my behavior or tell me what to do again. Jack can tell me not to go to the airport; heck, he can tell me not to do a lot of things. But the minute he does, I turn into a character from *Peanuts* and he turns into the teacher. All I hear when he talks is *Wah-wah-wah-wah-wah-wah.* Bardot was trying to behave while in Jack's eyeshot and not pull on the leash.

"Sally, didn't you say you wanted me to stop by to pick up that casserole dish I loaned you?"

"What? Who makes casseroles any mo—?"

"Of course you did, remember?" I said, linking arms with her as we walked past Jack, who was sitting on my front stoop. Bardot looked back, confused.

"You just ignored Jack. Don't tell me that you two are fighting?" Aimee looked shocked.

"We're not fighting yet, because I refuse to engage. He's angry that he told me to stay away from the drug bust and I didn't."

"Jack ain't the boss of you." Sally now had a cause.

"Oh Halsey, sometimes it's just easier to let them think they're in charge. Go back and talk to him, honey." I looked up and couldn't believe those words had come from Mary Ann. She was our journalistic trailblazer. Something didn't feel right.

"I say let him stew for a while. He should know by now that he can't tell you what to do," Peggy said. "Are we going to have to send him to summer school?"

I chuckled; Peggy has a way of doing that to me. We dropped Aimee off at her house and continued down the street.

It was still hot, but the afternoon sea breeze had started to roll in, and I couldn't help but think about a glass of chilled Sancerre. I hoped Sally had some on ice in her fridge.

"This is my stop," Peggy announced, "come on by if you change your mind about Wine Club. I'll open a bottle just in case."

"Bye Peggy." That feisty woman is truly remarkable.

"This is me," Mary Ann said. "Oh, and Jeb is home! See ya." She trotted off into her house.

"I've never been in their house, have you?" Sally asked me.

"No. I wasn't even really sure which one it was," I said and finally gave the exterior the once-over. And that's when I saw it.

"I'd hoped never to have to say this again Sally, but we need to call Augie."

"You're a glutton for punishment."

"I prayed this moment would never come," Mary Ann said, opening her front door.

"I'm so sorry, but I had no choice," I said, standing next to Augie and a uniformed officer. "I can leave Bardot outside if you want."

"We're going to need to come in and talk to Jeb," Augie explained, and she stood aside for us to enter. Mary Ann gave Bardot a little pat and waved her in. I'd also brought along Sally for moral support.

"Hey there guys," Jeb said, getting up from his recliner and turning off the TV. "I'm not sure how much help I can be. I take it you're here about Jonas."

"We are. Let's run through the events that led up to his death."

Augie took the armchair next to Jeb's and the rest of us found seats on the two sofas in the room. Mary Ann had disappeared into the kitchen, and I soon smelled coffee brewing.

"Jeb, you've said you hardly knew Jonas, but that's not exactly true, is it?"

He hung his head and shook it. "Jonas was helping me get medicines for the kids at the mission. He said he had a company that did this all over the world."

"Medications Without Borders, that's what they called themselves," Mary Ann said, bringing in the pot and several coffee mugs.

"But you figured out that wasn't entirely legit, didn't you, Jeb?"

"I probably knew all along and just turned a blind eye. I'd read a series in the *Times* about this mission and their uphill battle to help the neighborhood, and because I'd retired, I figured I could do some good for them. At first, I didn't know Jonas was the one running it. The packages would be sent to me and I'd take them down to Watts. I'd gotten an email explaining the delivery process and saying this was the safest way to get the medications into the right hands. I learned later it was also the safest way to protect the guilty."

"You're doing great, Jeb," I said, "and how did you find out that Jonas was involved?"

"Rusty."

"He just came up to you and told you?"

Augie really needed to get an imagination.

"Of course not. I like to have lunch at the Spitfire Grill. Mary Ann's always running somewhere with work and whatnot. One day, Rusty came in and asked if he could join me. We yakked for a bit, and then he slid a package across the table to me. *I think this is for you*, he said. Well, I figured the jig was up, but he promised not to tell anyone. He said he thought what I was doing was admirable. Rusty told me that Jonas was running this operation and said he was helping with another side of the business. He did say he hoped not for much longer. From then on, I swore to myself I would have Rusty's back."

"Enough so that you killed Jonas with a lethal dose of Devil's Breath?" Augie and the officer were watching Jeb very closely.

"Good God no. What kind of a person do you think I am?"

"Let Jeb tell his story, damn it!" came the loudest voice I'd ever heard Mary Ann use.

"Jonas had been fascinated with this Devil's Breath concoction. He'd grown up in South America and he convinced me it had all sorts of healing properties. That interested me because of the kids; some of them have very little hope of surviving. Jonas wanted me to make up a batch for him; he said he could use it in exchange for more medications. He took me to Rusty's hangar one day and showed me in a garden book what the drug was made from."

Sally and I nodded to each other. That had been the book we'd seen on our night raid.

"We never did check the age of that Spitfire card that was used to mark the page," Sally whispered. "We were going to get an idea of when it was done."

"No need now. We have our answer."

"It just so happens we have an Angel's Trumpet tree in our front yard. It's part of the same genus as the borrachero tree. Jonas knew I'd been a chemist. Rusty must have told him. He seemed to know what he was talking about, so I agreed to give it a try. Jonas wanted it in liquid form."

"You're admitting you created this Devil's Breath drug?" Augie was getting excited.

"For Jonas. Augie, weren't you listening?" Slowly, I could see the pieces falling into place. Jeb hadn't killed Jonas.

Jeb stood up from his chair, taking command of the room. I looked up at him, feeling his pain. He'd gotten up so abruptly that the recliner was still swinging, causing his hat to fall off the arm and onto the floor. It was his Australian bush cap.

"That was you arguing with Jonas in the hangar. It wasn't Jimmy!" I blurted out. "You guys are about the same height and have the same hats."

"Sweet Jesus, Mary and the Lord Almighty," Sally declared.

"What were you guys arguing about?" I asked when I'd regained my composure.

"I'd done some reading up on this drug since I'd given Jonas the vial of Devil's Breath. I'd had no idea how lethal it could be in the wrong hands. And Rusty had confided in me that Jonas wasn't the nice kid he gave off. He was refusing to let Rusty quit the drug distribution business. So, when I ran into Jonas by the museum, I told him that I wanted my serum back."

"I'll bet he didn't take that demand very well."

"No, Halsey, he didn't. In fact, he told me there'd been a change in the business plan and he'd no longer be providing me with medications."

"Sounds like we have means, motive and opportunity. This isn't sounding too good for you, Jeb," Augie said, while looking sympathetically at Mary

Ann. Somewhere below his beer belly, Augie had a heart.

"I know what it sounds like, but I didn't kill him, I swear."

"What happened after the argument, Jeb?" I prayed he would say something to exonerate himself.

"Jonas told me to go see Rusty and tell him to meet Jonas in the museum hangar at seven that night. I left to do as I was told. I couldn't stand to look at that guy for another minute."

The front door swung open and Jack stepped in.

"Here, sweetie, have some coffee and sit down. I made it just the way you like it," Mary Ann soothed to Jeb.

"Do you think Jonas was planning on killing Rusty, Jeb?"

He took a sip of his coffee and thought for a moment.

"I don't know that I had that much clarity, Halsey. I'd been so thrown by the argument. I'd never seen that side of Jonas. He was fierce."

"So, what did you do next, Jeb?" This time, it was Augie's turn to stand.

"I decided to go and sit in my car for a while and watch the planes take off and land. I must have drifted off into a deep sleep, because when I woke up it was dark outside."

"Jeb, think carefully. Do you remember much of what happened next?" I wanted him to take his time. I expected his next words would wrap this case up—if he could recollect enough of the evening.

"Not much really, although I will say that lately

some of the events are vaguely coming back. I got out of my car, realized where I was and checked the time. It was just about seven. I wasn't sure if I'd ever told Rusty that Jonas had wanted to meet with him, so I thought that I'd walk over to the museum to see if they had connected. When I got there, I saw there was a brick holding the door open. I walked in, but the museum was dark. I turned left into the hangar, which was where I'd left Jonas earlier in the day. The last thing I remember is seeing a light on in the flight simulator. I'm sorry."

"To be clear, you didn't have the Devil's Breath serum, Jeb, did you? It was still in Jonas's possession?" I asked.

"That much I know for sure, yes. But after that, it's a total blank, pretty much until I woke up the next morning in my own bed."

I breathed a sigh of relief and continued. "Mary Ann, you said that after Jeb's episode at Spitfire, when he was totally out of it and confused, he'd gone to the doctor and had a full battery of tests."

"That's right, and everything came back normal. Normal, that is, for someone who drinks and eats too much and doesn't exercise enough."

That got the men in the room to suck in their stomachs.

"Mary Ann, you told us that they were running one more panel to check for a substance in his blood they had seen traces of. Did you ever get the results of that test?"

"You know, I'd forgotten all about that. I probably put it on Jeb's desk, along with his other mail. Did you read the results, honey?"

Jeb shook his head and went in the other room to retrieve the envelope. The officer with Augie quickly followed him.

"Really, Augie?"

"Protocol," he stubbornly replied.

"You'd better read it, dear. I don't think I can hold the paper steady. This thing has got me so upset."

Mary Ann took the envelope, opened it, and first read it quietly to herself . . . then to the room.

"It says that the substance scopolamine was found in the patient's bloodstream. Enough that in a smaller man, there could have been a significant reaction. In a follow-up test a week later, there was no longer any trace of the drug."

"Jeb," I continued, "is it possible you entered the flight simulator to see if Jonas was in there and he was, waiting for Rusty? Did Jonas have a syringe loaded with Devil's Breath in his hand?"

"I guess so. I just wish I could remember." He shook his head in frustration.

"Augie, does it not seem to you that Jonas and Jeb fought in the cabin? Jeb got poked with the needle, and then, in defending himself, Jeb turned the syringe on Jonas and he got the brunt of the dose? The blood test proves Jeb had scopolamine in his system."

"When you put it that way, maybe. But Jeb could have conveniently chosen to lose his memory because he was the attacker rather than Jonas."

"Fine, have him take a polygraph, see a shrink, get hypnosis; these are certain to corroborate his story. And Augie, did you recover a syringe when your team searched the simulator?"

Augie nodded. "Yes."

"Then I assume you tested it for fingerprints. Did you find any?"

"Yes, Jonas's."

"No one else's? From, say, Jimmy or Jeb?"

"No. We were going on the theory that the killer wore gloves."

"If Jeb had been the killer, don't you think he would have taken the murder weapon away with him? He probably went for Jonas's wrist when he saw the syringe coming at him, which would be much easier to grab. This is a self-defense case." I'd said this with the vehemence of a preacher in a church full of whores.

"I still have to take you to the station to give a statement, Jeb. I'll get my supervisor involved and then see if we can let you go home on your own recognizance."

Jeb nodded solemnly. "I'll be right by your side," Mary Ann told him.

She went in the bedroom to get her purse and keys and the rest of us filed out. As I passed Augie, he touched my elbow.

"I will deny ever saying this, but that was some amazing detecting, Halsey."

"Your secret's safe with me. The only person I'll tell is Auntie Marisol."

"Don't you dare!" When I reached the sidewalk, Jack was waiting for me.

"I've worn the fight all out of me tonight, Jack. You'll have to save your tongue lashing for another day."

"Halsey, I'm sorry, I'm such a fool."

That wasn't exactly the response I'd expected,

given what he'd said to me earlier in the day. But I didn't say anything and continued walking to my house with Bardot.

"You were amazing in there," Jack went on, trying to keep up with me. He has much longer legs, but I walk like a New Yorker—fast and determined. "Heck, you were amazing throughout this entire ordeal. If you hadn't kept pushing and plowing away for the truth, heck, both Jimmy and Jeb might have been facing long prison sentences. You ran circles around the local cops, you even beat the DEA at their own game. You should be doing this, Halsey, for real."

I'd slowed down my pace.

"It was stupid of me to even try to tell you what to do, it's just that I love you so much that I can't help but be protective. In my bumbling, cow-on-ice way."

I couldn't help it. I laughed.

For the first time all day, I saw his face turn up in a smile.

"Can you see it in your heart to forgive me? Please?"

"Maybe. Now keep your voice down. Rose Avenue is trying to sleep."

We walked the rest of the way holding hands.

EPILOGUE

Things began to settle down on Rose Avenue. We were settling into autumn but still enjoying having events like Wine Club outside. Jeb's future was still hanging in the balance, but things were looking up for him and he was getting the care he needed. He was still working on recovering his memory and had made some breakthroughs. Augie so much as said to Mary Ann that Jeb's involvement in the case, along with the prescription medicine issue, would probably never even make it to the prosecutor's office.

"That's a relief. I think Mary Ann makes a fine addition to our Wine Club." Jimmy had also relaxed. He was back working with the good old boys at the airport and had taken up golf. To Bardot's delight, a neighbor two doors down had gotten a yellow Lab puppy for his son named Simba, and Bardot was showing him the pool ropes. And if that wasn't enough good news, I had made it my mission to plant something in the spot in my back-yard where the palm tree had been struck by light-ning. I went for a sago palm, which is still tropical but doesn't grow to biblical proportions.

Finally, the big day had arrived.

The Abigail Rose Winery looked a lot different from the last time I'd been there. It was clear Penelope and Malcolm had been hard at work not only getting it ready for planting season but for their beautiful, picturesque wedding as well.

The weather couldn't have been more perfect. Midseventies, the bluest of skies and a gentle, al-most whisper of a breeze. We'd heard Penelope's sister had flown in from London to be her maid of honor, and her parents were in attendance.

The dry rows of land we'd seen last time had been turned and fertilized and now sported young vine rootlings, getting accustomed to their new home. The stone house and tasting rooms had been spruced up and given a new roof and win-dows. We had gathered in front of it and toward the edge of the hill, where a gazebo and rows of chairs had been placed. Fall flowers were omni-present.

"Well, don't we all clean up good?" Sally re-marked, arriving with her husband, Joe, and cou-sin Jimmy. All three looked like they had just come from a Ralph Lauren catalog shoot.

Peggy had come with Aimee and Tom. She'd tossed aside the fleece and denim vests in ex-change for a dark blue midi skirt and a baby pink flared silk blouse.

Jack and I had made up, and he had kept his

promise not to try to tell me what to do. In return, it had dawned on me that it wasn't very realistic, when you're in a relationship with someone, to refrain from reacting to his or her decisions. We'd developed a new lexicon to soften our comments; if we weren't so comfortable with the other's choice in something, we would now say *okay, I'm here if you need me,* or *you know how to take care of yourself,* things like that. I still reserved the right to say, *You're wearing* that? if a certain ensemble seemed less than splendidly sartorial.

Speaking of which, it seemed our choice of wardrobe for the wedding was a success because every second person who talked to us asked if we'd set a date for *our* wedding. I'd gone with a knee-length, powder-blue-puff chiffon-tulle skirt and an off-white sleeveless shell. Jack wore a blue and white seersucker suit, white shirt and yellow-and-blue-paisley tie.

"Anyone met Penelope's parents yet?" I asked, scanning the lawn.

"Not yet. I'm not even sure what they look like." Aimee looked lovely in a floral print dress.

"Just look for the two people with the whitest faces and rosiest cheeks." Peggy was an anglophile and makes a pilgrimage to Oxford and Cambridge every year.

"Look, there's Marisol and her two girls." Sally waved them over.

Marisol also has a few items in her closet that aren't of the garden clog variety or culottes worn with holes. She'd gotten her hair done for the occasion and was even wearing heels.

"I was expecting you to fly in," I said to her.

"I thought about it. Hi Jack. You remember my girls, Martha and Terry?"

"I do, and all three of you look spectacular."

"Look, there's Malcolm!" Aimee clapped.

He was in white tie and tails and looked very handsome. I could tell he was nervous because his red cheeks were sending signals into space.

"I hereby declare the Rose Avenue Curse is gone! Come on, they want us to sit down." Sally herded us toward the folding chairs.

"We'll be right there," Jack said, steering me by the elbow to the other side of the tea roses.

"Halsey," Jack began, while lowering his six-foot-four frame down on one knee, "in the two years I've known you, my entire world has been turned on its ear in a much-needed way. You've taught me to be adventurous, take risks and laugh at life. You've shown me how to really enjoy people by letting my guard down and allowing myself to be vulnerable. Most of all, you've taught me how to love, unconditionally. After my dad died, I never thought I'd be able to open my heart like this."

He took a breath and reached into his jacket pocket. He pulled out a worn leather box with a gold clasp and opened it. Inside was the most gorgeous antique emerald-cut diamond engagement ring. It took my breath away.

I looked into his beautiful face and gorgeous amber eyes, looking up at me expectantly.

I really love this guy.

I got distracted for a moment when I saw a car driving up the curved path to the lawn.

"What on earth is Augie doing here?" I said.

What The Rose Avenue Wine Club Drank:

"Gibbs Obsidian Block Reserve Cabernet" Napa Valley, California

"Don Miguel Gasçon Malbec" Australia

"Bedrock 'Ode to Lulu' Rosé" Sonoma Valley, California

"Ciacci Piccolonini d'Aragona Ateo Red Blend" Tuscany

"Norton Reserva Chardonnay" Argentina

"Elyssia Cava, Pinot Noir Brut" Spain

"Tooth and Nail Fragrant Snare Chardonnay Blend" Paso Robles, California

"Paraduxx Rosé" Napa Valley, California

"Pittnauer Rosé" Austria

"Rideau Vineyard Rosé" Santa Ynez, California

"Mulderbosch Cabernet Sauvignon Rosé" South Africa

A Wine Club Guide to Pairing Wines with Cuisines of the World

A

American: Burgers and dogs don't always have to cry out for brewskis. In the summer there are actually a bevy of red wines that should be served chilled. Peggy, our Oregon wine aficionado, favors Johan Vineyards, Farmlands **Pinot Noir** from the Willamette Valley. She says that the Victoria plum and strawberry flavors with a peppery spice "make the burgers stand up and salute." For sausages and hotdogs I'm going to step in and suggest this Provençal-inspired **Rosé:** Liquid Farm Rosé of Mourvedre from Happy Canyon of Santa Barbara, California. Crisp, clean and refreshing, this gives a whole new meaning to "drinking a cold one."

Australian: If you've got some giant prawns on the barbie or are grilling Australian lamb chops, you'll want to top it off with some delicious Aussie wines. For the shrimp the Wine Club gals can't say enough about the Robert Oatley Signature Series Margaret River **Chardonnay** from Western Australia. Bright with white peach accents might have you declaring, "Strewth, this wine's bloody ripper!" For those beautiful, tender lamb chops Sally swears that the Aussies make the best **Shiraz.** She loves the Laughing Magpie Mclaren d'Arenberg **Shiraz/Viognier.**

B

Bavarian: Having a hearty meal of bratwurst mit sauerkraut? Throw on your lederhosen and pop the cork on a bottle of Airlie Winery **Riesling** from the Willamette Valley. It will stand up to the spiciest of mustards! And you know who loves sausage? Bardot!

Belgian: Penelope insists on eating her fries out of a paper cone whether they're made in Brussels or anywhere else for that matter. And her grape of choice for accompaniment? She says that you can't miss with a **Sauvignon Blanc** from France's Loire Valley and recommends a bottle of Les Deux Moulins for its dry, crisp flavor. Got waffles on your mind with powdered sugar and fresh berries? Then don't forget the sparkling **Vouvray**.

Brazilian: Feijoada, a hearty black bean kind of chili, is the national dish of Brazil. This stew is brewed with a variety of salted and smoked pork sausages and beef to make a rich and vibrant meal. And neighbor Argentina can provide the wine; a Bodini **Malbec** from Mendoza will do just fine.

C

Cajun/Creole: What's the difference between the two? It's a rural vs. urban style. Cajun is a more simple, stick-to-your-ribs cuisine with dishes like jambalaya, a one pot stew with rice and a base of browned meat, maybe alligator or shrimp. Wash it down with Sally's favorite Vivanco **Rioja** Reserva from Spain. If you add tomatoes to the jambalaya you can call it "Creole" but you'd be missing out on the classic Louisiana shrimp creole. Check out Paul Prudhomme's recipe and serve it with my choice of a chilled Eden Trail Eden Valley **Riesling** from South Australia to temper the heat of the dish.

Chinese: Is your moo shu pork feeling a bit naked? Add a glass of Jean Paul Brun Les Pierres Dorées **Beaujolais.**

E

English: How about a bit of bubbly with our fish and chips?" Penelope is known to ask. The affordable Scharffenberger Brut Excellence **Sparkling Wine** from Mendocino, California, is tip top!

F

French: The French have a wine pairing suggestion for every one of their signature dishes so it's hard to narrow it down. "If you're thinking that there is enough wine in a coq au vin then you're sorely mistaken, sister," Peggy once told me. I immediately ran out and bought some Maison Berthaude **Chateauneuf-du-Pape** from the Rhône Valley.

G

Greek: Who doesn't love a spanakopita spinach pie? Aimee is a huge fan and finds a reason to shout "Opa" every time she eats some. She also likes to pour some Ca' Momi **Bianco di Napa** for the table.

H

Hungarian: The next time that you dip into a bowl of chicken paprikash you might want to take a page out of Sally's book and decant a bottle of Langhe Nebbiolo **Barbaresco.** As she tells it you'll take one bite and one sip and say, "Ottoman!"

I

Indian: What goes best with naan flatbread, basmati rice and tandoori chicken? Penelope, who grew up in England, loves Indian food. For this smoky dish she recommends a fruit-forward **Pinot Noir** such as Stoller Dundee Hills from Oregon. Notes of plums, red currants and raspberries give it an earth-driven, plush finish.

Irish: Peggy's been known to tuck into a plate or two of corned beef and cabbage and not only on March 17. She's fond of a French white **Burgundy** with this dish such as a Genouilly Bourgogne Aligoté. "And for St. Pat's sake, don't dye it green!"

Italian: There is such a luscious bounty of great Italian food, but for now I am going to focus on pasta. If you like your noodles with tomato sauce I recommend a **Pinot Grigio** such as the Italian Tesoro della Regina, or for a red a fruit-scented **Nebbiolo** like the full-bodied Malabaila Roero Bric Volta from Piedmont, Italy.

J

Jamaican: Aah, Jerk chicken, red beans and rice, fried plantains and the dulcet sounds of steel drums. Pop open a bottle of the Portuguese white Fiuza **Avarinho** and you'll be sayin' "yah mon!"

Japanese: For sake's sake, try a rich red with your teriyaki and yakitori. Such as the Artezin Mendocino **Zinfandel** from California.

K

Korean: At a Korean BBQ of bulgogi and galbi sweet, smoky meats, Sally's partial to a Chilean **Syrah**, such as Casas Patronales Reserva.

L

Lebanese: Aimee's the one that introduced the Wine Club to Lebanese food. Now we're big fans of falafels, tabbouleh, shawarma, and the dish that

Sally can't say without giggling, baba ghanoush. But if this deliciousness has you scratching your hummus about what to drink with the meal, Aimee recommends a sparkling Levert Frères Cremant de Bourgogne **Rosé**.

M

Mexican: From your morning huevos rancheros to tacos and burritos to dark, rich mole, we like to sparkle! And no need to spend too much as you'll want many glasses with spicy food. Aimee's go-to choice is a Comte de Gascogne **Brut.**

R

Russian: We would never ask you to swap out your vodka with caviar, although you could do a wine chaser. But when enjoying Borscht or blini or beef stroganoff you can't miss with a glass or two of Peachy Canyon Incredible Red Zinfandel from California.

S

Soul Food: This is right up Sally's alley whether she's actually ever eaten true soul food or not. If she finds shrimp and grits on the menu she'll be looking over the wine list for a **Bourgogne Blanc.**

Swedish: It's a warm day and you've gathered outside for a light meal of gravad lax with a sweet mustard dill sauce and rye crisps. Time to break out the Banyan **Gewürztraminer** from Monterey County.

T

Thai: Intense spice begs for intense, full-bodied flavors in a wine. For that reason we recommend serving a nice **Grenache Blanc** with your Massaman curry, pad thai and larb.

V

Vietnamese: So, pho, a dish of salty broth, rice noodles that demand slurping with herbs and chicken or beef. Sally swears by the fizz from a glass of Famiglia Carafoli L'onesta **Lambrusco** Di Sorbara.

Connect with Us

Visit us online at
KensingtonBooks.com
to read more from your favorite authors, see books
by series, view reading group guides, and more.

Join us on social media

for sneak peeks, chances to win books and prize packs,
and to share your thoughts with other readers.

facebook.com/kensingtonpublishing
twitter.com/kensingtonbooks

Tell us what you think!

To share your thoughts, submit a review,
or sign up for our eNewsletters, please visit:
KensingtonBooks.com/TellUs.